ROUGH WATER

The swift current of the rampaging river snatched the raft, and it shot forward with a jerk, causing Nancy to stumble backward. Behind her, Joe whooped, "Here we go!"

"Hold on to your hats!" Frank shouted. As the raft plunged past the first line of rocks, he lunged with his pole to push the raft past a rock.

Suddenly their two prisoners started fighting, causing the raft to rock violently.

Nancy looked over her shoulder. "Stop it!" she yelled. "You're going to capsize us!"

It was too late. Even as she yelled the warning, the two men launched themselves at each other. Both of them fell over, landing on one corner of the raft. The flimsy craft tipped sideways.

Nancy let out a scream as all five of them were hurled into the churning white water!

Nancy Drew & Hardy Boys SuperMysteries

Available from ARCHWAY Paperbacks

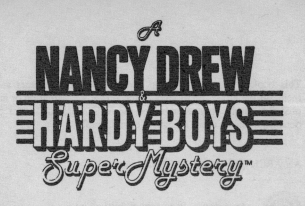

A NANCY DREW & HARDY BOYS Super Mystery™

HIGH SURVIVAL

Carolyn Keene

AN ARCHWAY PAPERBACK
Published by POCKET BOOKS
New York   London   Toronto   Sydney   Tokyo   Singapore

AN ARCHWAY PAPERBACK *Original*

An Archway Paperback published by
POCKET BOOKS, a division of Simon & Schuster Inc.
1230 Avenue of the Americas, New York, NY 10020

ISBN: 0-671-67466-8

First Archway Paperback printing August 1991

10 9 8 7 6 5 4 3 2 1

Cover art by Frank Morris

Printed in the U.S.A.

IL 6+

HIGH SURVIVAL

Chapter

One

"THE GUY'S FALLING!" George Fayne whispered, her voice filled with alarm. "He'll be killed!"

Nancy Drew sat up straight in her seat as George clutched her arm. "George, it's only a movie," Nancy returned in a low voice. "Take it easy."

George's attention was still riveted to the action on the TV screen. "Oh, he's all right. His safety rope held," she finally murmured. She let out a sigh, then turned to grin sheepishly at Nancy. "I know it's not real or anything, but I can't help taking it seriously. After all, we're going to be out scaling cliffs and stuff tomorrow, just like in that movie."

"Don't tell me you're sorry we signed up for

this Wilderness Trek course?" Nancy inquired in a whisper.

In the glow from the screen Nancy saw George shake her head emphatically. "No way! I wouldn't miss hiking through the Rockies for anything."

"I bet it'll be awesome," Nancy agreed.

Just then the film ended and the lights flickered on. Nancy blinked her eyes to adjust to the sudden brightness, then glanced around the small conference room of the Ramblin' Ranch Hotel, in Greville, Wyoming. She and George had traveled there that day from their hometown of River Heights to join a week-long Wilderness Trek program in the Wind River Range, a section of the Rocky Mountains.

In addition to George and herself, six other teenagers were in the room. They were all sitting in chairs that had been set up to face the TV monitor perched on a long table against the wall at the front of the room. As their group leader stepped up to rewind the video, a hum of conversation started among the group members.

"It's a good thing Bess decided not to come," George whispered to Nancy. "Hiking and rock climbing are definitely not her style."

"That's for sure," Nancy agreed, grinning at the thought. The only sports Bess Marvin was really interested in were shopping and dating. "But I bet she'll be kind of sorry she missed it when we tell her how cute the guys in our group are."

"Yeah!" George peeked appreciatively at the muscular, broad-shouldered guy to her right. Wavy, golden brown hair framed his square face and big green eyes. His name tag read Johnny Alvarez.

"It's too bad Frank and Joe Hardy didn't make the application deadline for the course, though," Nancy added. "They'd love this—"

"Ahem! Drew, Fayne," a voice barked. "If you'd cut the chatter for a few minutes, I'd like to wrap up this orientation session."

Startled, Nancy turned around. Their group leader was facing George and her, his hands planted firmly on his hips and his steel gray eyes flashing angrily. He was a burly man in his forties, wearing khakis and a flannel shirt. His short black hair was receding.

"Uh, sorry, Mr. Pemberton," Nancy said. "I didn't realize we were holding anything up."

Pemberton seemed to ignore her apology. "I hate to interrupt your conversation," he said, scowling, "but I'd like to get on with the trivial details of survival in the wilderness."

Nancy's blue eyes widened, and she exchanged a surprised glance with George. Why was Pemberton singling them out? They hadn't been the only ones talking.

Pemberton strode to the front of the room to face the whole group. "Now," he said, "the video you just saw should give you an idea of the obstacles you're going to be facing in the next week. The Wind River Range contains the highest mountains in Wyoming, and we're going to be climbing them. How many of you have done any rock climbing?"

Nancy raised her hand. "I've done a little," she volunteered.

"I have, too," George added.

Pemberton favored the girls with a sour smile, then turned his attention to the others. "Anyone else?"

It wasn't exactly the friendliest response Nancy had ever received, but she tried not to get annoyed. Checking out the others in the group, she saw that no one else had raised a hand.

"As I thought," Pemberton said with a nod. "Well, let me explain. The Wilderness Trek School does not offer live-off-the-land survival programs. We give you food supplies, camping equipment, and climbing gear. Still, it won't be a pleasure trip." He paused a moment for emphasis, then said, "We'll start out by plunking you down in the wilderness, bright and early tomorrow."

"Sounds good to me," a guy in front of Nancy murmured to the person next to him.

Pemberton went on to explain about the rough terrain, high altitudes, wild animals, and other hazards they'd be facing. "And don't forget, in the upper altitudes, above the timberline, there are permanent snowfields. It's not unheard of to have a snowstorm, even at this time of year."

"Wow!" George exclaimed softly.

"You're going to need a lot of strength, both physically and emotionally," the group leader went on. "Once we're on the trail, it's going to be impossible to turn back and go home. So if any of you are having second thoughts, you'd better make up your mind in the next twelve hours, while you can still back out."

He shut his mouth with a snap and gazed around the room. For a moment his eyes settled on Nancy, but she returned his stare calmly.

"Okay, lecture over," the group leader said after a moment. "You can pick up your gear outside in the hall. Oh—dinner tonight is at six-thirty at Buffalo Bill's. That's the steak-house next door. See you all there." Picking up a folder full of papers, he strode from the room.

As they all got up to leave, Nancy was glad to see that most of the group seemed to be as excited about the trip as she was. But when she glanced at Johnny Alvarez, he was actually scowling.

"Mr. Pemberton seems pretty tough," George commented to Johnny outside the conference room.

Johnny bent down to pick up a packet of

ropes and metal gadgets. "He's a good guy. You just have to know how to get along with him," he said.

"How do you know Mr. Pemberton?" Nancy asked.

"He's our football coach," Johnny replied, shrugging. "He works here summers. There's a bunch of us here from school for the course."

A pretty, black-haired girl suddenly appeared at Johnny's side. She was wearing jeans and a pink knit top. "Coach doesn't like know-it-alls," she said, giving Nancy and George a snide smile. Then she laid a hand on Johnny's arm.

George rolled her eyes at Nancy, and Nancy nodded. She was getting the distinct feeling that she and George weren't popular with some members of their group. She didn't know the reason why.

"Don't worry about it," said a voice on her left. "Coach is just a little prickly."

Turning, Nancy found herself facing a handsome guy with huge brown eyes, chiseled cheekbones, and cocoa-colored skin.

"Curt Walker," he said, holding out his hand. "You're Nancy Drew, right?"

"That's what my name tag says," Nancy replied, grinning and pointing to the small rectangle pinned to her T-shirt. "And this is George Fayne." Both girls shook Curt's hand. "I guess you're on the same football team, huh?" Nancy asked him.

"Fullback. My buddy Johnny here is our quarterback. A star, too," Curt told her. "Right, Johnny?" Johnny's only response was a tight nod.

"This is Melissa Somers, our head cheerleader, and her friend Stasia Kominsky." Curt gestured first to the dark-haired girl, then to a girl with pale skin and curly red hair who had come up beside Melissa. Her arms were filled with climbing gear. "We all arrived yesterday.

"Melissa's Johnny's girl. That's why she's here," Curt added. "And Stasia just goes wherever Melissa goes."

Melissa glared at Curt, then studied her long, pink fingernails.

"Uh, so what school are you all from?" George asked uneasily, trying to change the subject.

"Briarcliff. It's a private school near Chicago," Curt explained.

"We're from near there, too," Nancy told him.

Curt nodded. "I know. I've heard of you. You're a detective, aren't you?"

"Uh, yes, I am," Nancy said. She could feel herself blushing. Even though she'd solved dozens of cases, she was still embarrassed by the attention she sometimes received.

"You're big news at home. I read in the papers about how you and those two guys, the Hardy brothers, solved a diamond theft case

7

that had been baffling the Chicago cops for fifteen years," Curt said. "You're a local hero."

Nancy's blush deepened, and she was relieved when Johnny suddenly spoke up.

"We have stuff to do, Curt. Stop wasting time."

Curt raised his hands in a helpless gesture. "Guess I've got to go. See you two at dinner."

As the four Briarcliff students walked down the hall toward the lobby, Nancy saw that George's expression had darkened. "Wasting time!" she muttered angrily. "Who does that Alvarez guy think he is? What's with these people?"

"I don't know," Nancy replied, gazing after the group. "Maybe they're just a tight clique."

"Well, who needs them?" George snapped, but then she seemed to reconsider. "I guess we do," she said in response to her own question. "After all, part of this course is teamwork—"

George broke off as the other two guys in their program came out of the conference room. They both had straight shiny black hair and almond-shaped eyes. They looked to be a year or two younger than Nancy and George. From their name tags, Nancy saw that they were brothers, Dan and Pete Shimoya.

"I'm really psyched about this trip," Dan said after they had all introduced themselves. He was about Nancy's height, with hair cut short and a little spiky, and a compact athletic build. "Pete and I are from Cincinnati,

Ohio. We're both into hiking, but we've never had the chance to climb anything like the Rockies."

"Yeah," Pete put in. He was slightly shorter and a little heavier than his brother. "The biggest hills we get to see are the ones the ants make."

George laughed. "It's kind of like that where we're from, too." She picked up ropes and climbing equipment for her and Nancy while Nancy collected their tents and camping gear.

After talking to the Shimoyas for a few minutes, Nancy said, "Well, I guess George and I should head up to our room. I really want to check out all this stuff before dinner."

Leaving the Shimoya brothers to pick up their camping and climbing equipment, Nancy and George headed for the hotel lobby.

The Ramblin' Ranch was a small hotel, only three stories high. The lobby was a simple open room with a reception desk and a few couches and chairs. A wooden stairway led up to the rooms on the second and third floors, and an open doorway off the lobby led to the hotel restaurant. The place had a comfortable, woody feel. It seemed to attract people who liked the outdoors, judging from the ruddy-faced families Nancy had seen and the backpacks some of the other guests were carrying.

As Nancy headed for the stairs, George pointed to a soda machine in the far corner of the lobby. "I'll meet you up in the room," she said. "I want to get something to drink."

Nancy had been in the room for only a minute when a knock sounded at the door. She answered it and was surprised to see Johnny Alvarez standing there, looking uncomfortable. "Curt and I are next door. There's no soap in our bathroom," he explained. "Do you have an extra bar?"

"Sure." As she headed into the bathroom, Nancy asked over her shoulder, "Why didn't you call the front desk? I'm sure they have some."

"Hey, if it's a problem, forget I asked."

Boy, was he touchy! "It's no problem, really," Nancy called back hastily.

She searched around until she found some wrapped bars of soap in a small cabinet under the sink. When she walked back into the bedroom, Johnny was bending over George's sleek red backpack, which was leaning against the wall next to the room's small refrigerator.

"Nice pack," he commented.

"George always has great equipment," Nancy told him. "She's a real outdoors freak. And she's great at sports."

Johnny's eyes suddenly clouded. "Uh, yeah. Well, thanks for the soap," he mumbled. Then he turned and left.

Nancy sighed. She hoped the kids from Briarcliff would start acting friendlier once they were out in the wilderness. But even if they didn't, she was determined not to let them ruin her trip.

"I'm stuffed! I don't remember the last time I ate so much steak," Nancy groaned.

"Neither do I. It was a great dinner, though," George agreed, pulling open the front door to the hotel.

Nancy followed her friend inside and checked her watch. "It's only nine-thirty, but I'm beat. I think I'll go straight to bed since we have to get up so early tomorrow."

George gave an enormous yawn. "I'm ready to catch some *Zs,* too."

The girls took the stairs to the second floor, then walked down the long hallway to their room. As Nancy pulled the room key from her jeans pocket, she paused, sniffing the air.

"Do you smell smoke?" she asked.

George wrinkled her nose. "Now that you mention it, I do," she said, worry showing in her brown eyes.

"Uh-oh." Nancy thrust the key into the lock and threw open the door. A cloud of acrid smoke puffed out at her, making her cough. Instinctively she held one hand to her nose and flicked on the lights with the other.

"George!" Nancy cried. "Our room's on fire!"

Chapter

Two

Dense smoke was billowing out from around the small refrigerator against the far wall. Before Nancy's eyes a bright flower of flame blossomed and rose, scorching the wall and licking at George's pack.

"Nancy! My stuff is going to burn up!" George gasped.

Nancy had already moved inside the room. "Quick! Check the hall for an extinguisher!" she called over her shoulder.

In the meantime she'd have to try to put the fire out some other way. As George disappeared down the hall, Nancy turned back toward the fire. Still holding a hand over her mouth and nose, she snatched a blanket off the bed. She skirted the thickening smoke and flames near the refrigerator and ran to the bathroom. She soaked the blanket under the tub tap, then ran back into the bedroom.

Her lungs felt scorched as she breathed in the smoky air. Then the heavy, bitter scent of burning rubber assaulted her nostrils. It was now an electrical fire! If it got into the building's wiring, it could cause major damage.

A dull popping sound came from the back of the refrigerator, and Nancy had to leap back to avoid the shower of sparks that cascaded out. She shook the dripping blanket open and tossed it over the flames, crossing her fingers as it slid down between the back of the refrigerator and the wall.

The next thing Nancy knew there was a bubbling hiss. Then the lights in the corridor went out, and Nancy was plunged into total darkness! The only thing she could see was a fading glow where the fire had been. The entire hotel seemed strangely quiet, except for the hissing from the refrigerator.

"Nancy?" George's panicked voice came from the doorway, breaking the silence. "I couldn't find a fire extinguisher. Are you all right? What happened?"

It had happened so quickly that for a second Nancy wasn't sure herself. Then it hit her. "I guess I blew a fuse."

"I think you blew *all* the fuses," George's voice came back to her. She was chuckling softly. "I can't see a light on the whole floor."

"At least the fire's out," Nancy said. Spotting a single glowing spot on the floor, she stepped over and ground it out with her shoe. "It could've been really bad."

The sound of doors opening echoed up and down the corridor. "Hey, what happened to the lights?" Nancy heard someone complain.

"I'm coming in," said George. A second later Nancy heard a thud and a muffled "Ow!"

"Hold on," Nancy told her. "I've got a flashlight in my pack." She groped toward the foot of her bed, where she'd left her backpack, but her hands swooshed through thin air. "Hey, my pack's not here!"

"Mine's right here," George told her. Nancy heard her unzipping a compartment and fumbling inside. Then a strong beam of light sliced through the darkness. "Your pack's over here, near mine."

Nancy frowned. How did it get there? she wondered.

Just then the lights flickered on again.

"Oh, good," said Nancy, just making George out through the smoky air. "I was beginning to feel like we were in the Twilight Zone."

"Hey!" came Curt's voice. "I was just coming to see if you two knew what had happened."

Nancy turned to see the handsome football player framed in the doorway, Johnny right behind him.

"What's going on?" a new voice cut in. A

moment later Coach Pemberton appeared, pushing Johnny and Curt aside to face Nancy. A smaller man was with him. He had slicked-back black hair and wore a Western shirt and cowboy boots. He was the hotel manager, Nancy was pretty sure—she remembered seeing him in the lobby.

Nancy told them what had happened and concluded by saying, "I put it out by throwing a wet blanket over it. I guess I blew a fuse."

Pemberton's eyes grew wide. "Don't you know not to use water on an electrical fire?" he cried. "You tripped the circuits for the whole building!"

Angry color sprang to Nancy's face. "I didn't have much choice. The fire was spreading fast," she replied evenly.

"Girls!" Pemberton muttered disdainfully.

Nancy could see George bristling. "Maybe you would have preferred it if we *girls* had let the fire spread and the building burn down!" George said furiously.

"Please, let's calm down," the manager cut in anxiously. "Are you young ladies all right?"

"We're fine," Nancy assured him. She walked over and inspected George's pack. There was a scorch mark on the top flap, but otherwise it appeared to be undamaged. "Our stuff looks okay, too."

"Thank goodness," the manager said, obviously relieved. Then a questioning expression came over his sharp features as he pointed toward a plastic box affixed to the ceiling over the desk. "I don't know why the smoke alarm didn't go off. I'll have to have it checked."

As Nancy followed the manager's gaze, bells went off inside her head. "That *is* weird," she agreed slowly. She could hardly believe what she was thinking. No, it couldn't be. Could it?

"Maybe the battery's dead," Johnny said, shrugging. "No big deal. Everyone's okay, right?"

Nancy was barely listening to him. There was something she wanted to check out, and she didn't want the room full of people when she did.

"We're fine," she told the manager cheerfully. "Sorry to disturb you all. Now, if you don't mind, we need to get to sleep so we'll be in good shape for tomorrow."

The manager looked scandalized. "You can't stay in this room! It's full of smoke," he protested. "I'll put you somewhere else."

"That's all right," Nancy said in a firm voice. "We'd really prefer not to move. We're so tired we could sleep in the crater of a volcano. Right, George?"

"Uh—right," George agreed hesitantly.

It took some more arguing, but once Nancy opened the windows and the smoke began clearing out, the manager agreed to let them stay in the room. Finally everyone left, and Nancy was able to shut the door. She turned and leaned against it.

Facing her, George folded her arms and raised her eyebrows. "Okay, what's up?" she demanded. "Why did you want to stay in this room, Nan? I know when you're up to something."

Without answering, Nancy went to the refrigerator and tentatively touched it. Good, it had cooled. Reaching behind for the plug, she pulled it out of the outlet, then held the cord to examine it.

About an inch from the plug was a break in the insulation, with the blackened copper wire showing through it. The cord appeared to be very new, though. Nancy didn't know how the insulation could have ripped open like that, unless it had been cut.

"Earth to Nancy," George said behind her. "What are you doing?"

"I'll tell you in a second," Nancy replied. She put the cord down, then climbed up on the desk chair to examine the smoke detector. When she got the casing off, her eyes narrowed.

"There's no battery," she said, as if she hadn't been expecting one.

"Huh?" Then, seeing Nancy's face, George said, "Don't tell me you think someone did this on purpose so the alarm wouldn't go off? I mean, maybe the hotel staff just didn't get around to putting a new one in it yet."

Nancy replaced the casing and hopped back down to the floor. "I'm pretty sure the refrigerator cord was cut, too," she added, showing George. Then she went back and sat cross-legged on her bed. "I'm beginning to get the feeling someone doesn't want us along on this trip," she said soberly.

George still looked dubious. "Maybe it's just those kids from Briarcliff, pulling some kind of stupid prank because we're outsiders," she suggested. "I just can't believe the other two Wilderness Trek guys would actually try to hurt us. We don't even know them!"

Nancy gestured at her pack, which was still leaning against the wall next to George's. "I'm positive that when we left for dinner, my pack was at the foot of my bed. Now it's there. Someone moved it so it would be near the fire. Maybe the person figured that without our gear we couldn't make the trip."

George frowned. "I still don't get why someone wouldn't want us to come along."

Nancy propped her elbows on her knees and rested her chin in her hands. "Okay, let's think. Curt knows I'm a detective, so it's fair to assume the other Briarcliff students know, too. Maybe one of them has something to hide, something he or she is afraid I might find out on the trip."

"Like what?" asked George. "What kind of mystery could there be on a wilderness trek?"

"And who in the group is involved?" Nancy added.

George opened her mouth to say something

else, but instead she let out a huge yawn. Flopping down on her bed, she ruffled her fingers through her tousled brown curls. "Well, if I had to pick a villain, I'd choose Johnny Alvarez. He's cute, but he sure rubs me the wrong way."

"I was thinking the same thing," Nancy agreed. "He came in before dinner to borrow some soap. When I came out of the bathroom, he was bending over your pack."

"By the refrigerator?" George said, picking up on Nancy's reasoning. She turned to face Nancy, her eyes gleaming. "You mean he might have been tampering with the cord?"

"Possibly. It took me a while to find the soap, though I'm not sure it would be long enough for him to get the battery out of the smoke alarm," Nancy replied slowly. "I can't be sure yet. But I bet that whoever did this will try again. And if it is one of our climbing group, who it probably is, once we're out in the mountains, we're not going to be able to go to the police for help."

"So what should we do?" George asked.

Nancy thought for a moment. Then a smile spread across her face. "We need backup," she said, reaching for the phone on the small table between her bed and George's. "And I know just who to call."

"Wow!" George exclaimed. "These mountains are beautiful!"

"They're so majestic!" Nancy gazed in wonder at the peaks that rose above them in the early-morning light. They were covered with a blanket of evergreen trees that swept upward in dramatic folds. Far above, the trees ended abruptly at the timberline, and sheer granite peaks gleamed in the sunlight. Here and there Nancy could see the brighter glint of snow on the rocks.

Half an hour earlier she, George, and the rest of the group had piled into a van, which had brought them here to the foothills of the Wind River Mountains.

"I know we're only about ten miles from Greville, but it feels like we're a zillion miles from civilization," said a voice behind the girls.

Nancy turned to see Pete Shimoya standing by the pile of packs they'd unloaded from the van. He was wearing jean shorts and a T-shirt. A red bandanna around his forehead kept his straight black hair from falling into his eyes.

Pete's brother, Dan, raised his eyes from tightening the laces of his hiking boots. Letting out a low whistle, he said, "Now I see why the Indians call these the Shining Mountains."

The foursome from Briarcliff was standing off to the side. As Nancy glanced at them, Curt breathed deeply and pounded his chest.

"Mmm, fresh air. Makes me want to run all the way to the top." He turned toward Coach

Pemberton, who was sitting on a rock, and called, "Hey, Coach, where's the trail?"

Coach Pemberton grinned. "Trail? There is no trail, Curt. That would be too easy."

No trail? Nancy frowned. That was going to make it a lot harder for her "reinforcements" to find them.

Coach spread out a map on the grass in front of him, and everybody crowded around. "We're here," he said, pointing to a dot on the map. "And tonight we want to end up here." He pointed to a spot partway up a small mountain. Then he studied his group, his eyes taking in each face slowly. Nancy noticed that his gaze lingered longest on Johnny.

"I'll keep you pointed in the right direction, but it's up to you to get us there. You'll take turns leading, and, Alvarez, you're first."

"Whew! This is rough going," George panted four hours later. "I'm hot, and my pack must weigh fifty pounds. It's a good thing Tarzan up there is clearing the way for us." She jerked her head toward Johnny, who was easily striding through the woods with Coach Pemberton.

Nancy nodded breathlessly. Johnny had been a good leader so far, she had to admit. He'd found a deer track that helped them find a path through a particularly dense area of brush, and a couple of times he'd shifted fairly heavy tree trunks that had fallen across the way. There wasn't a marked trail, but he had found a path through the trees and rocks that was fairly clear.

Now, as she watched him, Nancy saw Johnny pause in front of an enormous boulder that blocked their way. Nancy could see that the path continued on the far side. She halted, curious about what he was going to suggest.

"Get out the machetes," Dan Shimoya joked as the others gathered behind the coach and Johnny. "We'll have to hack through the jungle to get around this baby."

Coach Pemberton leaned close to Johnny and spoke to him in a low voice. Nancy couldn't hear what he said, but after a moment Johnny bent down and set his right shoulder against the huge rock. Groaning, he heaved at it.

"He can't possibly budge that," George mumbled.

But it seemed he could. With a rumble the boulder moved! Then it rolled off the path, crashing into the undergrowth.

"Wow!" George cried in an admiring voice, and the rest of the group started cheering.

Johnny turned and grinned at them all, and Nancy was surprised to see what a friendly smile he had. Still, there was something that felt very wrong to her. The rock must have weighed hundreds of pounds! How had Johnny moved it?

As the others resumed hiking, Nancy hung back to check out the spot where the rock had been. After a moment she straightened up, her eyes wide.

Embedded in the ground were four stones shaped like a small pyramid, with a wide, flat stone capping it. The pyramid was so symmetrical, Nancy was sure it couldn't be a natural formation. Someone had put those stones there, then rolled the boulder on top of them, ensuring that it could be easily moved.

The obstacle Johnny had cleared was a fake!

Chapter
Three

$\mathbf{N}$ANCY STOOD THERE for a moment, staring down at the pyramid of rocks. Who had set that boulder in the middle of the path?

It must have been someone who knew the group would be coming that way—someone like Coach Pemberton. He knew the area well, and he had chosen Johnny as their leader that day. He could have planned for Johnny to move the fake obstacle.

Or Johnny himself could have set the boulder up. Maybe the reason he was so skilled in finding a trail through the thick undergrowth was that he already knew the route. He could have used ropes or even a log for leverage to hoist the boulder up on the small pyramid, she supposed. Curt had said that the group from

Briarcliff had arrived the day before everyone else. Though what Nancy couldn't figure was how Johnny would know where to set up the obstacle.

But why would either the coach or Johnny do such a thing? she wondered. And was there any connection between this and the fire in her and George's room the previous night? Nancy shook her head to clear it. Maybe she was just overreacting.

"Nan!" George called.

Raising her head, Nancy saw that the rest of the group had stopped and was waiting for her.

"Tired, Drew?" Coach Pemberton asked in a slightly mocking voice.

"No, I'm fine," she replied lightly. "I was just looking at something."

Was it her imagination, or did Coach's eyes narrow a tiny bit? Nancy couldn't be sure. All he said was, "Let's get going, shall we?"

As they resumed hiking, Nancy gestured to George to fall back with her. When they slowed to be about fifty yards behind the others, Nancy explained what she had discovered.

"I don't get it," George whispered, readjusting the strap of her pack over her jean shorts. "First someone sets fire to our room, and now you tell me our trail has been paved with fake obstacles. What's the point?"

"The two might not be related. . . ." Nancy

pointed out. Her voice trailed off as she cast a quick glance ahead. "Oops, we've got company."

"Hey, what are you two being so secretive about?" asked Curt, falling back to walk beside them. Flicking a spruce twig playfully at Nancy, he asked, "You're not on a case again, are you?"

Laughing, Nancy picked the twig out of her hair. "What gave you that idea?" she asked.

"Oh, I don't know. Maybe the way you keep looking at all of us, like you're wondering what crimes we've committed."

Nancy was relieved when Curt's attention shifted as they stepped out of the forest and into a meadow washed with brilliant sunshine. Letting out a whoop, he cried, "All right! Are we at the campsite already?"

The pine scent of the woods was replaced by the warm, fruity smell of larkspur. Nancy could see the flowers ringing a round pond in the middle of the field.

"Relax, Walker. We've still got a ways to go. This is where we stop for lunch," Coach explained.

"Oh, no, it's only lunchtime," Melissa said, groaning. "You'll all have to fix it without me. I'm pooped." She shrugged out of her backpack and plopped down on the grass.

"Me, too," Stasia echoed, doing the same.

Pemberton smiled indulgently at the girls.

"Coach doesn't seem to mind that they're

not helping," George commented, leaning close to Nancy. "I guess it's because they're part of his inner circle or something."

As Nancy and George set their packs on the grass, Pete Shimoya came over and sat down by them. He had taken off his red bandanna and was wiping his face with it. "I don't understand that girl," he commented, nodding toward Melissa.

Nancy shaded her eyes and peered at the pretty, dark-haired girl. Melissa had opened her pack and taken out two bottles of nail polish, one pink and the other a clear top coat. Now she was applying a fresh coat of pink to her long nails while complaining to Stasia about how the morning's hike had ruined them.

"You mean you wonder what she's doing on this trip?" George asked wryly.

Pete raised his eyebrows. "Seems like she'd be happier shopping or getting her hair done."

"Or getting a manicure," George added.

It was true, Nancy thought. Melissa didn't seem the type to enjoy roughing it. "But you know, she doesn't seem to be having trouble with the terrain. She didn't lag behind at all," Nancy said. "And even though she's complaining, she doesn't look tired."

"Yeah, and I know why," Pete put in. "This morning I heard her sweet-talk Johnny and Curt into carrying most of her gear for her."

"Curt?" George murmured. "That's weird. I

had the impression he and Melissa didn't get along."

Pete shrugged. "I don't know the guy, but he seemed happy to carry ten pounds of tent for her."

"Who knows? There's some complicated stuff going on among those four," Nancy said.

After they'd rested for a few minutes, the coach called the group together. He showed them how to choose a bare patch of ground or a flat rock on which to build a twig fire. Then he instructed the teenagers to split into two groups.

The Briarcliff students stuck together, so Pete and Dan Shimoya ended up with Nancy and George. The four of them gathered twigs for their small fire. Then Nancy and Dan set up a tripod to hang their soup pot on, while George and Pete sliced apples they'd carried in their packs.

"Mmm, those smell great!" Nancy exclaimed as she caught the scent of the fruit. "Let's get this soup going!"

Dan stretched his muscular frame as if to get the cricks out after the morning's strenuous climb, then bent down and picked up the soup pot. "I'll get some water from the pond."

"I wouldn't," Coach called. "Even up here the pond water may not be safe to drink. Can anyone tell me why?"

There was silence. Then George spoke up.

"Because it's still water," she suggested. "It might have harmful bacteria in it."

Nancy grinned at her friend, but she noticed that the coach didn't seem to share her approval. In a grudging tone he muttered, "You're right, Fayne." Addressing the group in general, he added, "Stick to your canteens for now. There's a spring near tonight's campsite. We can fill up then."

After lunch was cleaned up, Coach Pemberton gave the group a lesson in reading the topographic maps. He had them take landmarks from the terrain to figure out where they fit in on their relief maps. He was a good teacher, Nancy had to admit. He really seemed to know the Wind River Mountain Wilderness, and it was obvious that he loved it. She could see why the Briarcliff students were fond of him, but she still didn't understand why he was being so unfriendly to her and George.

After about an hour they shouldered their backpacks and moved on. Judging from the sun, and from what they had just learned, Nancy knew that they were traveling from southeast to northwest, along the mountain's western face. They were still well below the timberline.

Coach Pemberton had told them that rock climbing wouldn't start in earnest for another few days or so. Still, now that they were getting deeper into the mountains, the terrain was becoming more challenging.

"Phew, I nearly lost it on that last stream," George commented as she joined Nancy on the far bank of a swift-flowing stream. She glanced back to where Stasia was hopping precariously between two boulders.

"Me, too," said Nancy. She peered into the dark green shadows ahead of them. "I wonder how much worse it gets."

About half an hour later they found out.

"How are we going to cross that, Coach?" Curt asked. Nancy heard the dismay in his voice, though it was partly drowned out by a loud noise.

Coming up behind him, Nancy saw that Johnny and Curt and the coach had halted at the edge of an especially treacherous-looking stream that rushed furiously below. It had carved out a deep gorge between two rocky cliffs.

"Good question," said Coach Pemberton, smiling slightly. "In a situation like this we use a mountaineering technique called the Tyrolean traverse."

"What's that?" Melissa asked.

Beside her, Stasia made a face, brushing her curly red hair back. "I think we're about to find out."

"That's right," Coach replied. "I need a couple of volunteers." He clapped Johnny on the shoulder. "Alvarez, I know you want to try this. Now, who else is game?"

For a moment there was no sound except the

rushing of the stream below. Then Nancy raised her hand.

"All right, Drew, if you insist," the coach said heavily. "Listen up," Pemberton went on. "It would be a waste of time and effort for everyone to rappel down this side of the gorge, ford the stream, and then climb up the other side. Does anyone not know what *rappel* means?" Stasia reluctantly raised her hand.

"It's a way of going down a cliff using a rope to support yourself. So here's what we're going to do. One person will rappel down and climb on over."

He flicked a thumb toward Nancy. "You've had a little experience, Drew, so that person will be you. Once you're on the other side, you'll secure your rappelling rope to an anchor—a sturdy tree or a protruding rock—on the other side of the river. Then Alvarez will attach himself to that rope by hooking up a seat sling and a carabiner—you all have these in your climbing kits."

Pemberton held up a metal ring in the shape of a C with a metal catch covering the small open portion. He showed them how to slide back the catch so that the carabiner could be clipped onto a rope. "The carabiner attaches you securely to the rope, yet it slides to give you freedom of movement," he explained.

"Alvarez will haul himself hand over hand to the other side of the gorge," Pemberton went on, "bringing with him a belay line. We'll use the line to pull the rest of you and your bags safely across in your seat slings. Belaying is any one of several methods to prevent you from falling to the end of your rope. Got it?"

Everyone nodded soberly.

Following the coach's instructions, Nancy clipped herself into her sling. She tied the ends of her rope together so that it formed a big loop, then draped it over a big fir. The loop stretched below her to the bottom of the gorge. Then she attached her sling to the rope and began her descent. Using the rope as a pulley, she rappelled, letting her weight carry her down and relying on the friction of the rope against her sling shackles to keep her from going too fast.

The cliff was sheer and almost vertical, which made it easy to rappel. In no time Nancy was at the bottom. Cautiously she forded the rushing stream, then climbed up the opposite side. The cliff there had a relatively gentle slope and plenty of handholds.

That was easy! Nancy thought with a rush of triumph. She reached the top and tied both ends of her rope securely around a thick, gnarled root that stuck up from the ground. When she was done, she waved to Johnny, signaling that it was all right for him to begin crossing the gorge.

The noise of the rushing water made it impossible to hear the group, but Nancy could clearly see the nervousness on Johnny's face.

She didn't blame him for being scared. The distance was only about thirty feet, but a fall would be deadly.

She watched as Johnny put on his sling and clipped the round aluminum carabiner to the sling and the traverse rope. Coach tied the belay line—the rope that would be used to pull the others across the gorge—to his sling. Then Johnny started across. Nancy held her breath as he inched closer, dangling from the sling and pulling himself hand over hand. His eyes, she saw, were clouded with raw fear.

"You're almost across," she called encouragingly to him. "It's just another few feet. Come on, you can do it!"

Finally he was a bare eight feet away. "What do I do now?" he asked in a tight voice.

"Reach out with one hand and toss me the belay line," Nancy told him. "I'll pull you in."

Cautiously Johnny let go of the traverse line with one hand. He gave Nancy a determined grin and reached for the rope that was tied to his sling. And then it happened.

Johnny's carabiner suddenly gave out, releasing his sling. He let out a yell as his body swung free.

Nancy gasped, her heart pounding. Johnny was hanging by one hand, dangling high above the raging torrent! If he let go, there was nothing to keep him from crashing to his death on the rocks below!

Chapter

Four

"DON'T PANIC, JOHNNY!" Nancy called to him, but she could see her words had no effect.

"Help!" Johnny's face was perfectly white, and complete terror was in his eyes as he looked up at her. "Help me!"

Nancy sucked in her breath. From across the gorge the coach was yelling something, but his words were swallowed up by the roar of the rushing water below. It was up to her to do something—and fast!

Her gaze lit on the useless sling Johnny was still strapped to and the rope that the coach had attached to it. "Can you toss me one end of your belay line?" she called to him. "I think I can pull you in."

"I-I'll try," Johnny said. He reached slowly with his free hand for the rope that was tied to his sling. The loose end dangled a half-dozen feet below him; Nancy held her breath as his groping fingers found the rope. She didn't know how long his right hand could support the weight of his body. Faster! she urged him silently.

Sweat streamed down Johnny's pale face as he slid the rope through his left hand to get some slack. Then he tossed it to Nancy. She leaned out, straining to catch it, but the throw was short! The rope passed a foot from her fingertips, then dangled uselessly from Johnny's sling.

"You almost made it. Try again," she encouraged him. "Remember, you're a quarterback. You're good at throwing things."

Johnny didn't smile. Wordlessly he retrieved the rope. After taking up the slack, he tossed it again.

Nancy grabbed hold of a sapling and let herself lean as far out over the gorge as she dared. She snatched at the belay line as it soared by. "Got it!" she called.

Without wasting a second she pulled herself back to a firm footing, wrapped the line around a big aspen, and began to haul. She pulled the rope until it stretched in a straight line across the gorge, then she tied it off. Now if Johnny's hold on the traverse line slipped, he wouldn't plummet to the bottom of the gorge. The belay line, still attached to his sling, would catch him.

Nancy walked back to the edge of the cliff. "Okay, Johnny, you're anchored to the belay line now, but you still have to make the last few feet hand over hand. Come on, now. You can do it."

Gritting his teeth, Johnny reached up with his left hand and grabbed the traverse line. It seemed to take forever, but at last Johnny was at the edge of the cliff, groping for a foothold. Finally his feet were firmly on the cliff.

"You did it!" Nancy exclaimed.

He took three shaky steps before his knees gave out and he collapsed. "Thanks," he croaked. "You saved my life. I nearly killed myself out there!" Suddenly his whole body was trembling.

Nancy put a hand on his shoulder. "You didn't nearly kill yourself," she said softly. "It wasn't your fault. There was nothing you could have done about it."

"That makes it worse!" Johnny moaned.

Nancy wasn't sure what he meant, but she realized he was probably in no condition to talk rationally. Reaching down, she helped Johnny out of his sling. She was about to toss it aside when something about the broken carabiner caught her eye. She peered at it more closely.

The aluminum catch was bent outward. Near its base there was a patch where the metal looked stressed and worn, as if the catch had been bent back and forth several times.

Nancy's eyes narrowed. Was it sabotage? Had someone deliberately weakened the metal so Johnny's carabiner would break? Something about that didn't make sense, though. One minute Johnny had been set up to look like a hero by moving the huge boulder so easily. The next minute he had been set up to be killed!

Maybe the incidents weren't connected, though, Nancy reminded herself. She was about to show the carabiner to Johnny, but his white face told her that then was the wrong time. He'd had enough shocks for one day. She casually tucked the carabiner into her backpack. Then she took out two of her own and fastened them to Johnny's sling. She'd look into the sabotage later.

One by one the rest of the group hooked their slings to the traverse and belay lines, and Nancy pulled them across. Coach Pemberton was the last to cross. He seemed genuinely concerned as he rushed over to Johnny and congratulated him on his handling of the crisis. He didn't say a single word to Nancy, though.

Melissa was positively cooing over him, Nancy noticed, though he seemed too dazed and withdrawn to notice her. It seemed as though Melissa really did like Johnny. Nancy had wondered about their relationship after seeing them together and hearing how Melissa manipulated him and Curt.

"Hey, Nan, that was nice work," George congratulated Nancy, coming up beside her.

"It sure was," Dan Shimoya chimed in. "You were great! We were all riveted, watching how you saved him."

"I'm just glad Johnny's okay," Nancy told them. As Dan went over to Johnny, Nancy tugged on George's sleeve to separate her from the others. Nancy filled her in on the possible sabotage of the carabiner. "We've got to keep our eyes and ears open," she finished. "You and I may not be the only ones under attack. It looks like someone's after Johnny, too."

A low whistle escaped from George, and she shot an anxious look toward the others. "I hope our backup arrives soon," she said. "It sounds like we're going to need help."

That was another worry. Nancy had avoided thinking about it all day, but now she voiced it. "I don't think we should count on them. We're hiking over pretty rough terrain, and there's no marked trail. We have to assume they may not be able to find us.

"What a fantastic place!" George said, grinning.

"I'll say," Nancy agreed. After unbuckling her waist band, she shrugged her pack off and looked around.

They had finally arrived at the place where they would camp for the night. It was a wide, sloping meadow that gave them a sweeping vista of mountains bathed in the reddish glow of the late-afternoon sun. At the lower end of the meadow, tall, graceful lodgepole pines fringed a small stream that fed into a crystal-clear lake. Except for the rustling of a breeze in the treetops, the place was absolutely silent.

"Hey, Coach, can we swim in that lake?" Johnny asked, pointing at the sparkling water.

"I don't see why not," Coach Pemberton replied. "You might find it cold, though. It's snow runoff."

Johnny had been moody and silent after his near-fall at the gorge, but now his face became animated and he lit up in a brilliant smile. He let out a whoop, then yelled, "Let's go!" at the same time as he peeled off his T-shirt.

Curt, Dan, and Pete quickly followed. In a flash all four boys had tossed aside their T-shirts, socks, and boots and were racing toward the water in their hiking shorts.

Nancy looked questioningly at George, who nodded eagerly.

"Let's do it!" George exclaimed.

The two girls grabbed their bathing suits and ducked behind some bushes to change. Approving whistles greeted them as they ran to the lake. Nancy grinned. They were just wearing one-piece racing suits, Nancy's in aqua and George's in red, but the suits probably looked glamorous compared to the dusty shorts and T-shirts they'd been hiking in all day.

"Oww!" Nancy cried as she splashed into

the water. It was the iciest water she'd ever been in, but after the first shock wore off, it was deliciously refreshing.

"Think fast, Fayne!" Pete cried. He swept his hand through the water and sent a thick spray over George.

"Ooh!" George squealed. "You asked for it."

She sent a return splash at Pete, but her aim was bad and she got Johnny instead. "Oh, sorry," she called. She gave Nancy an apprehensive glance. Johnny was so moody, there was no telling how he'd react.

Johnny just burst out laughing. "That calls for revenge," he said, and dived in the direction of George's feet.

After that the water battle was on. Even Stasia and Melissa jumped in. Melissa didn't seem very happy about all the attention Johnny was giving George, Nancy noticed. And George definitely seemed to be warming up to the moody football player.

This trip might be an adventure—in more ways than one!

"What did you say that constellation was?" Dan Shimoya asked, pointing to a group of stars arranged in an elongated cross.

"That's Cygnus, the Swan, and the brightest star in the group is Deneb," Coach Pemberton told the group.

They had already cleaned up after a dinner

of fried potatoes, dried beef, and a special protein soup. The night was crisp and clear, so the group of teenagers had laid out their pads and sleeping bags in the open air near the fire, rather than put up their tents. Coach Pemberton had set up his tent, but he was still outside, pointing out the summer constellations.

"I could sit here and look at the stars forever," Nancy murmured to George. They were sitting cross-legged on the ground, a little to the side of the other kids, their flashlights on the ground beside them. "I don't think I've ever seen them so bright."

"Mmm, even though it is kind of cold," George said, rubbing her hands against the thick wool of her sweater. "Coach wasn't kidding about how fast temperatures can change."

A definite chill had settled in the air as the sun set, and everyone in the group had changed to long pants and heavy sweaters. Nancy had also put on a red windbreaker over her cableknit sweater to protect her from the wind.

Suddenly George let out a gasp that made Nancy jump. "Nan," she whispered, "I just saw someone's shadow. There are people out there watching us!"

Nancy felt her body tense. "Where?"

"There, by that big tree," George said, pointing.

Nancy grabbed her flashlight and stood up. "Let's check it out," she whispered.

The two girls crept away from the fire as silently as they could. Nancy kept her flashlight switched off, not wanting to alert whoever was out there that she and George were onto them.

They crept toward the edge of the field, and then into the forest. Instantly it grew pitch dark. "George, stay close to me," Nancy whispered. "We don't want to be separated."

"I'll bet—" George began. Suddenly her words turned into a muffled shriek.

Nancy whirled. "George!"

Then an arm snaked out and around Nancy's throat from behind. A strong hand was clamped firmly over her mouth.

Chapter

Five

Nancy's heart was pounding. In the inky darkness of the woods, she couldn't see her attacker, and his grip was too strong for her to break.

Thinking fast, she let her body go limp, pretending to faint. Whoever was holding her didn't loosen his grip. Instead, Nancy heard only a soft laugh in her ear.

"Nice try, Drew," said a familiar voice. "But don't forget, I've seen you use that trick before."

The hand over her mouth was lifted away. This time Nancy really *did* feel weak in the knees as surprise and happy relief washed over her. "Frank Hardy!" she exclaimed softly.

"In the flesh," he replied, releasing his hold on her throat. "We've been trying to get your attention for the past fifteen minutes, but you were too busy playing astronomer to see us."

In the dark Nancy heard scuffling noises off to her left. "Ow! George, it's me, Joe Hardy!" came the muttering voice of Frank's younger brother. "But I won't let you go if you don't quit biting!"

"Joe?" came George's breathless voice. "Oh, sorry!"

With a soft chuckle Nancy switched on her flashlight. Joe, dressed in jeans and a red polo shirt, still had a restraining arm around George, and his wavy blond hair was a little disheveled. Frank was looking on, an amused expression in his brown eyes. He was a year older and had a taller, leaner build than Joe, with dark hair and intense brown eyes. Nancy picked out their backpacks propped against a tree a few yards away.

"Our backup," Nancy said, grinning as Frank swept her into a bear hug.

"It's great to see you!" they both said at once, and their excited whispers turned to soft laughter.

"Hey, Nancy. Hey, George!" Joe greeted them, keeping his voice low. He gave each of them a kiss on the cheek. "Yes, your reinforcements have finally arrived."

"And how!" George put in, rubbing her shoulder. "This is one reunion I'll never forget."

"I was afraid you guys wouldn't be able to

find us," Nancy said. A smile crept over her face as she glanced at Frank.

Though Ned Nickerson would always be the guy she loved with all her heart, Frank Hardy was still special to her. She and Frank understood each other so well. Maybe it was because they were both detectives. They were definitely on the same wavelength, to the point where they often found themselves finishing each other's sentences.

"Well, it was a chase," Frank said in answer to Nancy's comment. "We caught a red-eye flight to Salt Lake City, then hopped a plane to Jackson last night, and got into Greville about an hour after your group left this morning. We managed to find out where the hotel van took you—"

"Without making the manager too suspicious," Joe put in.

"And then we followed your trail," Frank finished. "That was the hard part. For a big group you guys didn't leave much in the way of tracks."

"Come on, Frank, it wasn't that hard," Joe protested. "We were great!"

George laughed. "That's for sure!"

"How's everything in River Heights?" Frank wanted to know. "How are Bess and Ned doing?"

"They're both fine," Nancy told him. "Ned's getting ready for fall semester at Emerson, and Bess is putting in long hours perfecting her tan. She'll be sorry she missed you two. Especially you, Joe," Nancy added with a sly grin. Joe and Bess weren't involved romantically, but they were both outrageous flirts—particularly with each other.

"Hey, it's my fatal charm. Women are all over me like flies," Joe retorted.

Frank hooted. "Like flies on a rotten apple, that is. Little brother, your modesty never ceases to amaze me." He turned to Nancy, brushing a lock of dark hair off his forehead. "So, want to tell us what the big emergency is?"

"It keeps growing," Nancy began, thinking of all that had happened since the fire in their hotel back at Greville. "Let's get comfortable—it may take a while to tell you everything."

George glanced anxiously into the dark woods surrounding them. "We'd better talk fast, though, so we can get back to camp. They've probably missed us already."

The four teenagers made themselves comfortable on the pine needles that blanketed the ground at the base of a huge evergreen tree. Keeping their voices low, the girls repeated to Frank and Joe the story of the fire in their hotel room the night before, then told them about the possibly sabotaged carabiner that had caused Johnny's accident at the gorge and the strange tensions among the Briarcliff clique.

"Nan, don't forget to mention how Johnny

was set up with that fake obstacle today," George chimed in. "That was really weird."

Nancy explained what had happened. Her voice became thoughtful as she added, "But I'm not sure he was set up. He might have done the setting up himself."

"He wouldn't!" George said instantly. Then, as if embarrassed, she glanced down and began to sift through the pine needles.

"What makes you so sure?" asked Nancy, raising her eyebrows and peering at George. "Just last night you told me you thought Johnny would make a good villain."

Without raising her head, George mumbled, "Well, maybe I was wrong about that. He's not entirely awful." She dropped a handful of pine needles and suddenly became very interested in retying the laces of her hiking boots.

Nancy couldn't help smiling. George was definitely developing a crush on Johnny. Nancy just hoped it didn't get too serious. It didn't seem as if Melissa would take kindly to competition.

Aloud, she merely said, "We can't rule Johnny out until we know more about what's going on. Don't forget, he's the best candidate for having set the fire in our room. And he could have done the other things, too."

"Even sabotaging his own carabiner?" George asked in disbelief. "Why would he do that? Nan, he could have died!"

"Maybe it was some sort of bizarre cry for attention," Nancy said, shrugging. "I don't know. The point I'm trying to make is, we don't know enough yet to make any real judgments."

"Nancy's right," Frank put in.

"Whew!" Joe added, shaking his head in amazement. "It sounds like there are a lot of unsolved mysteries here! From what you've told us, there might be three separate cases—tracking down whoever set that fire in your room and finding out who's responsible for setting up that boulder and the attacks on your pal Johnny." He grinned easily. "It's a good thing you called in the pros."

"There he goes with his macho act," George retorted, rolling her eyes. "You sound like Coach Pemberton."

"Who is this coach?" Frank inquired.

Nancy wrapped her arms around herself to keep the cold out. "He's another complication. Coach Pemberton is our group leader. He's also the football coach at Briarcliff—that's where half of our group goes to school. He doesn't seem overly fond of either me or George—"

"Ha!" George cut in. "That's the understatement of the year."

Frank steepled his fingers, and furrowed his brow while he concentrated. "Hmm, it all sounds pretty complicated. Maybe Joe and I should keep out of sight for now. Your group would be suspicious of us if we just showed up suddenly."

"Besides, we may be able to learn more if no one knows we're here," Joe put in.

"Do you have enough warm clothes and food?" George asked.

Joe grimaced. "If you count trail mix and dried fruit as food, we have enough to last us a year. But if you guys cook up any bacon cheeseburgers in your camp, I wouldn't mind if you sneaked a few our way."

"I'm afraid most of what we have is pretty dull, too. Powdered soup mix and stuff like that," Nancy told him, laughing.

"Ugh!" Joe said with a look of horror.

"Hey, Nan, we'd better get back to camp," George said, tapping the face of her watch. "We've been out here for forty-five minutes."

"Wow, I had no idea," Nancy replied. She got to her feet and dusted off the seat of her jeans. "You're sure you'll be all right?" she asked Frank and Joe anxiously.

Frank smiled up at her. "We'll be fine. Joe's right about one thing—we really were dying to come on this trip. Your call was just the excuse we needed to tag along."

"Glad to hear it," Nancy replied, smiling back. It was just like Frank to act as though she and George were doing *them* a favor, instead of the other way around. "Well, sleep tight and stay close. George and I will try to check in with you at least twice a day."

"We should arrange some sort of signal," Joe suggested. He raised a teasing eyebrow. "How are you girls at hooting like owls?"

George reached out and ruffled Joe's blond hair. "Forget it."

"I think it would be easier if we just set a target time," Nancy suggested. "Let's say that you should look for us about a half hour after we break for lunch and also at about nine-thirty every night."

"Sounds good," said Frank, and Joe nodded his agreement.

"Great, then it's settled," Nancy replied. She and George said their good-nights, then turned and made their way quietly back to camp.

When they got there, everyone else was asleep, their sleeping bags radiating out in a circle around the fire. A lantern was lit in Coach Pemberton's tent, and Nancy could see his silhouette. He seemed to be writing on a pad or clipboard.

"It's so peaceful," George whispered to Nancy as they plopped down on their sleeping bags.

Nancy nodded. The only sounds were the chirp of a few crickets, the hiss of the fire's dying embers, and the faint crackle of a radio from the coach's tent. Across the fire from George and her, Nancy saw Melissa stir and shift, reaching to adjust something at the foot of her sleeping bag, near the flames.

Nancy looked away to stare up into the soft, dewy night, but a moment later a loud crackling noise drew her attention back to the fire. The pyramid of charred sticks in the pit had collapsed, sending a shower of sparks shooting up into the air.

Those guys are awfully close to the fire, she thought, glancing worriedly at Melissa, Stasia, and Johnny in their sleeping bags. The feet of their bags were no more than twelve inches from the glowing embers of the fire. She didn't want to awaken them unnecessarily, but on the other hand . . .

Nancy was just about to call over to the threesome when a pillar of flame suddenly whooshed up.

"Oh, no!" Nancy cried, her eyes widening.

The flames had spread like a shot to the foot of Johnny Alvarez's sleeping bag. It was on fire!

Chapter

Six

NANCY JUMPED to her feet. She heard George gasp beside her. "Come on!" Nancy said urgently.

The two girls raced around the fire. "Johnny, wake up!" George shouted as they reached him. She gave his shoulder a violent shake.

"Huh? What's going on?" Johnny mumbled. Then his eyes focused on the flames at his feet.

"Aaagh!" he yelled, sitting bolt upright in his sleeping bag. In one fluid motion he threw himself backward, out of the bag.

Nancy seized the bag and swiftly flipped it over to smother the flames. She stomped on the bag until she was sure the fire was out. George joined her a moment later with canteens she must have gathered from the others.

Together they doused the sleeping bag with water.

"That should do it," Nancy muttered, finally noticing the other kids who had crowded around the charred sleeping bag. The coach was just emerging from his tent.

"What happened?" Melissa asked.

"A log in the fire collapsed, and I guess a spark caught Johnny's sleeping bag," Nancy replied. She didn't see him. "Johnny, are you okay?"

There was no answer. "Johnny?" Nancy stepped away from the fire and then saw him, sitting some distance away on a rock.

"Are you all right?" Nancy asked, going over to him. "Did you get burned?"

Johnny gave her a shaky smile. "No, I'm all right. You must be my guardian angel, Nancy. How can I ever thank you?"

"You could hire me as your bodyguard and pay me an enormous salary," Nancy joked. After that accident she figured he could use a laugh.

Johnny just buried his face in his hands. "That's the second time today," he moaned. "I should never have come on this trip. I guess it's true—I *am* jinxed."

George had come up during this speech. Now she laid a hand on Johnny's shoulder. "That's ridiculous!" she told him fiercely.

She turned to Nancy, and with a subtle nod

of her head gestured toward the edge of the campsite. She wanted to talk privately with Nancy.

Before the girls could move away from Johnny, though, Coach Pemberton came over, followed by the rest of the group. "Alvarez, how did it happen?" the coach asked anxiously.

"I don't know, Coach." Johnny lifted his head from his hands and gave Pemberton a weary look. "I went to sleep, and the next thing I knew, Nancy and George were yelling at me to wake up, and my sleeping bag was on fire. I didn't even feel anything through the insulation." Shaking his head, he added, "I could've been turned into a human barbecue if they hadn't come along."

Melissa gasped and ran to put an arm around his shoulder. "Johnny, don't say that!"

No matter how unpleasant she was in other ways, Nancy reflected, Melissa did seem to be there for Johnny when things went wrong. George must have noticed, too, because she shifted her gaze to stare down at the ground.

"So it was you two again?" Coach Pemberton said, interrupting Nancy's thoughts. She saw him scowling at George and her. "Well, well. Fires do seem to follow you around. And how did you happen to see this one start?"

Nancy could hardly believe what he was

implying. They'd saved Johnny's life, and the coach was practically accusing them of setting the fire! She counted to ten to calm her anger.

"Uh—we heard a whoosh when the bag went up," Nancy replied evasively. She didn't want to lie, but she wasn't about to draw attention to the fact that she and George had been up and out. If Coach knew about that, he'd want to know why. He might start keeping an eye on them, and that would make it a lot harder to keep in touch with Frank and Joe.

"It's a good thing they were still up, isn't it, Coach?" Melissa chirped in a sweet voice. "I saw them come back from the woods right before the fire started." As she spoke, the cheerleader was gazing at George with a gleam of malicious satisfaction in her eyes.

She did that on purpose! Nancy thought, furious. She wanted to get us—or at least George—in trouble.

It seemed that Melissa had succeeded. Coach Pemberton's nostrils flared angrily. "Drew, Fayne—in my tent," he barked. "I want to talk to you! I'll be there as soon as I see what I can do for bedding for Alvarez."

Nancy and George exchanged a questioning look as they walked toward Coach Pemberton's tent. "Fires do seem to be a theme on this trip. I'm still not sure how this one got started," Nancy mumbled once they were in the coach's tent.

As she and George took a seat on the ground, George gripped her arm excitedly. "That's what I was about to tell you, right before everybody else came over!" she said, her voice vibrant with excitement. She peered through the open tent flap to make sure no one was in hearing distance before whispering, "Nancy, there was kerosene on Johnny's sleeping bag. I smelled it!"

Nancy's mouth fell open. "Are you sure?"

"Positive," George answered, nodding so vigorously that her dark curls fell forward onto her forehead. "After you went to see if Johnny was okay, I shook out his sleeping bag so it would dry faster. There was a funny smell besides the smoke." She leaned forward. "I'm telling you, it was kerosene!"

Nancy's gaze lit on the kerosene lamp that illuminated the inside of the coach's tent. "But Coach Pemberton has the only kerosene lamp—" Nancy broke off, shaking herself. "Hold on, Drew. Let's not jump to conclusions. Someone else could have gotten hold of the kerosene. Or Coach could have accidentally spilled a few drops from his lantern."

"It's possible that someone else could have gotten hold of it," George agreed. "But don't tell me it was an accident, Nancy. After what happened today at the gorge—"

She broke off at the sound of approaching footsteps. A moment later Coach Pemberton stepped into the small tent, bending low to fit through the opening. The tent was only about four feet high, and the coach seemed like a giant inside it. He sat down cross-legged on his sleeping bag.

"I've had about enough of you girls!" he bellowed, glaring at Nancy and George.

Nancy could feel George start beside her.

Moderating his voice, the coach went on. "We're supposed to be acting as a team. But your know-it-all attitudes and now this irresponsible midnight jaunt are ruining any team spirit."

Nancy stared at Coach Pemberton in amazement. Know-it-all attitudes? She and George had helped save Johnny. And hadn't her part of crossing that gorge been part of a team effort? "I don't understand," Nancy said after a short silence.

"You think you can do anything!" the coach ranted on. "You think you're the best! Well, let me tell you, I won't allow you to destroy the morale of the other members of this group."

Suddenly a light flashed on in Nancy's mind. "By 'other members of this group,' you mean Johnny Alvarez, don't you?" she asked the coach.

He blinked, obviously taken aback. "What if I do?" he blustered after a minute.

Nancy frowned. "If you don't mind my asking, why are you so concerned about

Johnny?" she asked. "What's wrong with him?" She lowered her voice, not wanting anyone to overhear.

"That's none of your business," Coach snapped.

"It might help us understand what we're doing wrong," she pointed out, trying to be patient.

The coach stared back and forth between Nancy and George. His face was red, and he seemed to be struggling to overcome his own annoyance. "All right," he said after a moment. "Alvarez was my star quarterback."

"Was?" Nancy repeated.

"That's right." The coach sighed heavily. "Was—until last year. He had a rough fall in a scrimmage. His helmet came off, and someone's cleat just missed his eye. It spooked him. Then a few days later he threw a bad pass, and the kid who tried to catch it ran off the field and into a ditch that happened to have some rusty metal in it. The kid cut himself badly and ended up getting blood poisoning and going to the hospital.

"Alvarez decided it was his fault," the coach concluded, shaking his head. "He lost his nerve. And that made us lose games."

"But it wasn't his fault!" George protested. "He didn't force the other player to run off the field like that. And it's not as if he put that metal in the ditch or anything."

"I know," Coach Pemberton replied. "But

Alvarez doesn't see it that way. There have been other incidents, too—a car accident that injured his sister and some smaller things. Anyway, Alvarez is convinced he's a jinx. He thinks he's dangerous to himself and anyone who's around him."

So *that* was what Johnny had meant when he said he was jinxed, Nancy thought. Her heart went out to him. "Poor guy," she said softly.

"He doesn't need your pity," the coach growled. "Do you think that'll bring his confidence back? Not likely! Why do you think I organized this trip? I want him to conquer the mountains."

Suddenly what he was saying made perfect sense to Nancy. Staring directly into the coach's eyes, she said, "That's why you set up that phony boulder incident, isn't it?"

Coach Pemberton's face flushed bright red, and he glared at Nancy. "So what if I did," he sputtered at last. "He's got to learn to believe in himself again, and I'm helping him. The last thing he needs is a couple of girls showing him up by doing it all better than he can!"

George and Nancy exchanged a startled glance. "Maybe you're looking at it the wrong way," Nancy suggested, trying to be tactful. "There's no reason Johnny should feel threatened by me and George, just because we're girls. And we really haven't been trying to show off—"

"Don't give me that," Pemberton interrupted. "What about that stunt today at the gorge? You were glad when Alvarez fell and you could stage that spectacular 'rescue.'"

Nancy was shocked. Coach was completely twisting what had happened!

"That's absurd!" George burst out. "You're just lucky Nancy was there! Otherwise, whoever rigged that carabiner to break would have succeeded, and Johnny would be at the bottom of that gorge!"

The coach was staring at George as if she were speaking a foreign language. "What are you talking about?"

Nancy took a deep breath. She hadn't meant to tell him, but it was too late now. His surprised reaction to the sabotage could just be an act. If so, maybe she could goad him into slipping up.

"I didn't stage what happened at the gorge," Nancy said in a firm voice. "But you're right about one thing—*somebody* did. The carabiner had been weakened by someone. Also, the fire this evening may not have been an accident, either," she continued. "George smelled kerosene on Johnny's sleeping bag."

Coach's eyes narrowed to slits. "Are you trying to say that—"

"Coach Pemberton," Nancy said quietly, "I think someone is trying to put Johnny out of action—maybe for good."

Chapter

Seven

"THAT'S RIDICULOUS," said the coach after a moment of shocked silence. "Who here has any reason to hurt Alvarez?"

"I don't know," Nancy admitted. "I was hoping you could answer that."

Pemberton shook his head. "Of course I can't. Who did you have in mind? Walker? They're teammates. None of my players would knowingly hurt another one."

"What about Melissa?" George asked. "Would she harm Johnny?"

"Alvarez's girlfriend? That girl worships the ground he walks on," the coach said impatiently.

Nancy nodded. That much seemed to be true. "How about Stasia?" she asked.

"She and Melissa are best friends. Stasia wouldn't do anything to harm Melissa's boyfriend." Coach gave a short, humorless laugh. "Face it, girls. Nobody's trying to hurt Alvarez. You've been reading too many detective stories."

"But—" Nancy began.

Coach held up his hands. "End of discussion. Now, get on out of here and go to bed."

After leaving the tent, Nancy and George walked out of earshot of the coach's tent. They found a log and sat down on it.

"If you ask me, Coach himself is behind Johnny's 'accidents,'" said George.

"It's possible," Nancy agreed. "I can't imagine why he'd want to put his own quarterback out of commission, but there could be things we know nothing about."

"I guess we can rule out Pete and Dan," George added. "They never met Johnny before this trip. That doesn't give them much of a motive."

Nancy nodded. "Not necessarily. But everyone else has to be considered a major suspect." She rested her chin in her hands and thought about it. "I wonder about Curt," she said. "I haven't noticed any great warmth between him and Johnny. Maybe he's jealous of the attention Johnny gets. We should keep an eye on everyone, though. Even the two Shimoya brothers. There may be a connection that's not obvious."

Yawning, Nancy added, "We'll start tomorrow, though. For now, we'd better get some sleep. We need to be on our toes for whatever happens next."

"So much for blue skies," George commented the next morning, staring straight up.

Nancy finished tying her sleeping bag to her backpack and stood up, brushing a few strands of damp reddish blond hair off her face. "That's for sure," she agreed.

Ragged clouds raced overhead, propelled by a strong, gusty wind that blew up the mountain. The air was warm but humid, and Nancy, George, and the others were wearing their rain ponchos. One brief, heavy shower had already taken them by surprise as they were breaking camp.

"Ouch! These mosquitoes are driving me crazy!" Dan Shimoya slapped at his neck as he propped his pack against the log where Nancy and George had sat the night before.

Beneath the plastic hood of his poncho, Dan's almond-shaped eyes were serious. "Hey, I hope you guys didn't get in too much trouble last night. It didn't exactly seem fair."

Nancy smiled at him. "We just got a lecture about being better team players. Nothing too serious."

"You guys have been great so far," Dan told them. "If anyone needs a lecture on team spirit, it's the kids from the coach's school.

They've barely said two words to Pete and me."

Nancy squinted toward the lake, where the four Briarcliff students were standing in a loose huddle by the water's edge. Johnny was waving his arms and talking forcefully.

"What are they up to?" she wondered aloud. As she watched, Curt, Melissa, and Stasia turned and headed back toward the campsite. Johnny stayed behind, staring out over the water, while the other three made a beeline for Coach Pemberton, who was still dismantling his tent.

Nancy, followed by George and Dan, wandered closer to the group from Briarcliff, just in time to hear Curt announce, "Coach, Johnny's dropping out of the program. He asked us to tell you that he's not going to finish the trip with us."

Nancy sucked in her breath. That was news!

"What?" Coach bellowed. He dropped the tent and ran across the meadow to where Johnny was standing.

"Hey, what's going on?" Pete asked, brushing his black hair off his face as he joined Nancy, George, and Dan.

Nancy decided to let Dan explain the situation to his brother. "We overheard what you said," Nancy told Curt, stepping over to him. "Did Johnny say why he's dropping out?"

"He can't hack it," Curt replied, swatting

nonchalantly at a mosquito. "He thinks he's under a curse or something."

Nancy couldn't help noticing that Curt didn't seem too dismayed by the news. In fact, he seemed to be faintly satisfied. "What do *you* think?" she pressed.

Curt shrugged. "I think he should quit if he wants to."

"Don't tell me you think he really *is* jinxed?" George asked, frowning.

"If you believe something hard enough, you can make it come true," Curt said, shrugging again.

Just then Melissa and Stasia stepped up to them. "Why are you so interested, anyway?" Melissa asked, peering suspiciously at Nancy and George.

"Yeah, it's really none of your business," Stasia added, brushing back her red hair.

"We're worried about Johnny, which is more than you three seem to be!" George answered hotly. "Besides, we're a *group,* remember? Something like this affects all of us—it's everyone's business."

At that moment Coach Pemberton came striding back from the lake, his poncho flapping in the wind. "I can't talk to the kid," he said, throwing up his hands. "He won't listen!"

Nancy and George exchanged glances. "Excuse us," Nancy murmured. She and George headed for the lake. Johnny was sitting on the sodden bank now, skipping flat stones across the water.

"Hi," George said softly. "Can we join you?"

Nancy thought his eyes brightened a little when he saw George. "Hey, it's my guardian angels," Johnny said in a tired voice. "Sure, have a seat.

"I guess you heard the news," he went on as Nancy and George sat down on either side of him, using their ponchos to protect them from the wet grass.

Nancy folded her long legs in front of her and clasped her arms around them. "We heard," she replied. "Johnny, you're making a mistake. If you quit, you'll wonder for the rest of your life whether you would have made it if you'd stuck it out."

"There's no point in sticking it out!" Johnny cried. "Didn't you hear what I said last night? I'm a jinx! If I stick around, I'll bring trouble on everyone."

"That's garbage!" George burst out angrily. "It's plain old superstition, and I can't believe you're giving in to it. If those guys were really your friends . . ." She trailed off, her brown eyes flashing with indignation.

Johnny stared at George as though he'd never really noticed her before. "You have really nice eyes," he said suddenly.

"What?" George said, obviously caught off guard. Her mouth opened and shut a couple of times, and her cheeks turned bright pink.

Johnny blushed, too, Nancy noticed. He looked as if he couldn't believe what had come out of his mouth. Nancy had a feeling George had just given Johnny a reason to go on with the trip. Nancy had another reason.

"I'll tell you this, Johnny," she said briskly. "You'll never make it back to town on your own."

Johnny's jaw was set stubbornly. "I found the way here, didn't I?" he said. "I'll make it back."

Nancy didn't see any reason to tell him that Coach Pemberton had been partly responsible for that. "Even though you're jinxed?" she asked.

"I—" Johnny broke off, looking startled.

Nancy laughed at his expression. "Come on. George and I know you're not jinxed. But whether you believe us or not, you have a much better chance of making it through these mountains if you stick with the group. We're your guardian angels, remember?"

Johnny shifted his gaze from Nancy to George, and then back to Nancy again. Finally the ghost of a smile appeared on his lips. "Okay, you win."

"All right!" Nancy and George cried together, giving each other and Johnny a high five.

Then the three of them walked back to where everyone else was waiting and informed them that Johnny had changed his mind.

Dan and Pete were the only ones to cheer, Nancy noticed with surprise. Curt turned away, annoyed. Melissa, with Stasia behind her like a pale shadow, stepped up to Johnny, Nancy, and George. Glaring at George, she took Johnny's arm and pulled him firmly away.

Coach Pemberton merely clapped his hands and called sharply, "We've wasted enough time. Let's get moving!"

"What's going on?" George mumbled to Nancy as they shouldered their packs and set off. "You'd think they'd be glad that we got Johnny to change his mind. It's as if they're all in on a giant conspiracy to get rid of Johnny, and we're the ones ruining it."

"In which case we'd better watch our backs," Nancy added in a low voice.

"Shake a leg, folks," Coach Pemberton called after they had stopped in the shelter of a rock to eat a quick lunch of cold, soggy sandwiches. "We've still got a good hike ahead of us."

It had continued to rain off and on for most of the morning. They had gained more altitude and were now near a rocky ridge where the trees were thinner and the ground muddier. The muscles in Nancy's legs ached from the

previous day's hiking, and her boots kept
slipping. Her jeans and boots were soaked
through, making every movement even more
tiring.

Nancy and George exchanged a worried
look. There was no way they could get away to
talk to Frank and Joe.

Finally at about four o'clock, the rain
seemed to let up. But the wind gathered force,
moaning through the trees, and thunder began
to rumble faintly behind them.

Up ahead Nancy saw Coach glance anxiously at the sky. As if in response, a jagged bolt of
lightning suddenly arced down just yards
away, striking a fir tree. The tree split open
with a crack, and a loud clap of thunder
boomed.

An instant later it was as if the sky had
turned into a vast, upside-down ocean. Rain
poured down in sheets, driven sideways into
the group's faces by the wind.

"Oh, great!" George yelled in Nancy's ear.
"If we don't get struck by lightning, we'll get
swept away in a flash flood."

Coach Pemberton signaled everyone to
gather in a huddle. "We can't go on in this!" he
shouted. "Too dangerous. We'll have to find
shelter."

"Where?" Stasia yelled, her eyes filled with
fear.

"Follow me," the coach told them. "There's
a cave nearby that'll give us some protection.

But no one is to go inside until I've checked it out. Wild animals often use caves as lairs."

"Wild animals!" Melissa wailed.

As the group set off again, Nancy adjusted her poncho so that a trickle of rain that had been funneling down her back now ran off her shoulder. She stared at the muddy mountain.

I hope we didn't lose Frank and Joe in this rain, she thought. I hope they're all right.

"This was a great idea, Joe!" Frank yelled over the pounding rain. The mud sucked at his hiking boots, fighting each step he took. "Just terrific! Got any more? Like maybe setting up a lightning rod and seeing if we can zap ourselves dry?"

"Well, you didn't have to agree with me when I suggested we try a shortcut!" Joe yelled back.

Frank clamped his mouth shut. He and Joe were negotiating a treacherous, muddy slope littered with loose pieces of rock and very few trees. A sharp overhang gave them some protection from the rain—except when the wind shifted and lashed stinging drops into their faces.

They'd had little difficulty in keeping up with Nancy and George's group, but the going was rough and tiring. When the group leader had started climbing a steep, lengthy rise, Joe had rebelled.

Frank replayed the conversation in his

mind. "Let's take a shortcut," Joe had suggested. "We know where they are now, and we know they're heading northwest. It'll be a piece of cake to hook up with them again. All we have to do is cut behind that low peak there."

Frank had had his doubts, but he hadn't wanted to climb the slope, either, so he'd gone along with Joe. Now they were struggling along in mud that was already up to their ankles and getting deeper fast. Lightning flashed all around them, and thunder shook the ground.

Joe paused to push a lock of soaked blond hair out of his face. Then he cocked his head, and Frank saw a wary expression cross his brother's blue eyes.

"Uh, Frank—do you hear something?" Joe asked. "Like a low, constant rumble?"

"That's thunder, genius."

"I don't think so," Joe said. "It's more— Hey! Frank! Look out!"

Frank's head snapped around, and then his eyes went wide. "Mud slide!" he yelled.

The overhang above their heads was collapsing. It seemed as if the whole mountainside were racing toward them, quivering and rumbling. If he and Joe didn't get out of there fast, they'd be buried alive!

Chapter

Eight

RUN!" JOE SCREAMED. He started racing down the mountain as fast as his legs would take him. He didn't need to look to know that Frank was with him—and that the wall of mud was only a few hundred feet behind!

"We'll never outrun it!" Frank yelled to him.

Joe's heart was pounding as he scanned the distance below. "That gully!" he shouted back. "We've got to cross it!"

He pointed to the right, where a runoff stream had carved a deep gully into the mountain. If they could get to the other side, the streambed might act as a channel and siphon off the mud.

Frank nodded, and they took off for it. Risking a glimpse over his shoulder, Joe saw that a churning wall of mud, boulders, and uprooted small trees and brush was racing after them. It would be just a matter of minutes before it steamrollered over them!

Joe poured on more speed. He and Frank covered the hundred yards to the streambed in record time. Joe paused on the lip, peering across the rushing torrent of water. "It's more than fifteen feet across!" he yelled in dismay.

Beside him Frank peered quickly up and down the bank. "There!" he cried, pointing to a slender laurel sapling that leaned over the edge of the gully. "That's our bridge!"

Joe and Frank raced to the young tree. "You first," Joe panted. He cupped his hands into a stirrup for Frank's foot.

Frank stepped in, and Joe boosted him up the trunk, but the tree bent only slightly. "I'm not heavy enough!" Frank called down. "You'll have to climb up, too. Joe—hurry!"

Joe didn't need any encouragement. He practically flung himself up the tree, backpack and all. The muscles in his arms strained and bulged as he pulled himself higher. Again the tree swayed but not enough for them to drop to the far side of the gully.

Before Joe could catch his breath, the churning waves of mud were on them, racing by just a few feet below the fork in the laurel where he was wedged. As he had figured, the torrent of mud and debris was channeled down the gully, but there was still no way for them to cross it!

"I guess we're stuck," Joe called up to Frank,

who clung to the trunk about a yard above him. "This tree is tougher than it looks."

"Let's hope it's tough enough," Frank replied, letting out a sigh of relief. For a second there, he'd thought Joe was a goner. Frank squinted up at the sky. The thunder and lightning had let up somewhat, but the rain was still pelting down.

Raising his head to scan the sky, Frank glimpsed something black racing through the sky about a mile to the northeast of where they were. What was a little two-seater plane doing out in this weather? Pointing, Frank hollered, "Joe, look!"

The small plane was losing altitude fast—it was clearly in trouble. As he and Joe watched, it skimmed the treetops, then dipped almost out of sight. It appeared to have been heading for a granite cliff.

"It's going down," Joe said, wincing.

Frank tried to follow the course of the plane, but he was jolted just then as a huge boulder slammed into their tree with a big *kaa-runch!* A bone-jarring shudder ran through the slender trunk, and the laurel began to sway.

"Uh-oh," Frank muttered. "I think we're going down, too."

"Whoa!" Joe yelled. "Lean toward the gully!"

Clinging with his hands and feet, Frank threw his weight to the tree's right side. Joe swung out below him at the same time. For a moment they simply hung there, suspended in midfall. Then, with quivering slowness, the tree began to topple.

"Look out below!" Frank cried. He had a dizzying glimpse of sky, trees, and then ground rushing up to meet him. The impact was surprisingly gentle, though, cushioned by the branches of the falling tree.

"Well, it wasn't exactly the crossing I had in mind," said Joe as he and Frank climbed out from under the branches. "But we made it."

Frank checked out his sopping, mud-streaked clothes. "And we're only slightly the worse for wear," he said, grinning. Then he sobered. "Come on, let's go. We have to get to that plane. Whoever's in it might need help."

Joe nodded, and they set off with Frank leading the way toward the granite face where he'd last glimpsed the small plane. They'd barely started, though, when an orange glow appeared in the dim sky, then faded. Seconds later a faint booming reached their ears.

"That wasn't thunder," Joe said grimly. "I think that plane just blew up."

Frank's jaw tightened. "We should keep going, though. It's been over ten minutes since we last saw the plane. Maybe the passengers had a chance to get out before it went up."

They slogged through the mud and rain, which had now slackened to a steady drumming. Lightning still flared, but Frank noted that the intervals between the flash and the crack of thunder were getting longer. The storm was retreating.

After about an hour's climb the Hardys emerged into a clearing. Joe, who had taken the lead, stopped short. "Oh, no," he muttered.

Frank felt a tightening in his gut as he made it to Joe's side. At the far end of the clearing he could see the remains of a small propeller plane, its wrecked fuselage wedged up against the base of a steep, rocky slope. Dark smoke drifted up from a gaping hole in the side. One wing was still connected, but the other was on the ground, several yards away.

Moving quickly, they split up as they approached the plane. Joe went around to the left while Frank stopped to peer in through the hole. Shreds of wiring and scorched insulation dangled from the ceiling. By some freak chance the control panel looked almost intact.

Frank was about to take a closer look when he heard Joe call, "Over here! I found someone!"

Heading around the plane, Frank saw Joe bent over a heavy, dark-haired man in jeans, a green plaid shirt, and hiking boots. He was sprawled on his back near the edge of the clearing.

"I don't see any blood," Joe reported.

Suddenly the man's eyes fluttered open. They were a pale blue, in contrast to the ruddy coloring of his face. His pupils dilated, then shrank to pinpoints as he struggled to focus.

Frank knelt by the man's side and pulled out his canteen. "You're okay, buddy," he said. "Have some water."

"Wha—" the man said thickly. A wild look flashed into his eyes. "Who're you?"

"We're friends," Joe said soothingly. "Take it easy. We saw your plane go down, and we thought you might need help."

"Plane . . ." The man lifted his head weakly and gazed at the wreckage. Then he fell back. "Five o'clock. Don't be late," he whispered.

"Sir, was there anyone else with you?" Frank asked urgently. "Any passengers?"

"No. Alone," the man murmured. Suddenly he clutched at Frank's arm. "I have to get out of here!" he said clearly.

Frank and Joe exchanged glances. "Uh, I don't think we should move you," Frank told the man. "You might have internal injuries or broken bones we don't know about."

An agitated grimace contorted the man's face. He flapped his hands and struggled to sit up. "Late, late," he gasped. "Let's go now!"

Joe shrugged. "Well, whatever's wrong with his mind, it looks like his back isn't broken," he told Frank in a low voice. "We probably should move him someplace more sheltered."

"Definitely," Frank agreed.

At that moment a male voice rang out in the nearby woods. It was answered by a higher voice that sounded even closer. "Hey, that was Nancy!" Frank exclaimed.

The voices seemed to jolt the pilot wide awake. Grabbing Joe's shoulder, he pulled himself to his feet, his pale blue eyes wild with fear, his face a sickly greenish gray color. He tottered, and Joe held on to his arm.

"Let's go now," the pilot hissed through white lips.

"Let's do it," Frank agreed. The guy was so upset it was probably better to go along with him, for the moment. If it turned out he needed medical help, they could always join Nancy's group later.

Supporting the pilot between them, he and Joe half carried him out of the clearing. After they'd gone a short distance into the woods, Frank and Joe led the pilot over to a moss-covered boulder and propped him up against it. Frank pulled his younger brother aside.

"I'm going back to the clearing to see if I can talk to Nancy," he said. "I think we have to make a change in plans—this guy needs a doctor."

"Okay," said Joe. "I'll watch him."

Frank hurried back to the clearing and paused just out of sight. He watched as Nancy, George, and a couple of guys walked up to the plane.

"Wow, check this out," a slim, dark-haired kid said, pointing at the hole in the fuselage.

Then a big guy with sandy hair spoke up. "I wonder what happened to the pilot?"

Frank turned his attention to Nancy. She wasn't listening to what the others were saying. Instead, she was methodically circling the site, her eyes on the ground. Looking for tracks, Frank realized. She doesn't miss a trick!

Almost as if she'd heard him, Nancy turned and started moving toward him. Her face, framed by her poncho hood, was taut with concentration, her blue eyes narrow. When she was a yard away, Frank whispered her name. She started slightly when she heard him, but she didn't say a word. She just continued to move casually into the forest.

As soon as they were out of sight, Nancy grabbed Frank's arm. "I thought we'd lost you guys in the storm," she said in a hushed whisper.

"You almost did." Frank told her about the mud slide and how they'd climbed the tree and spotted the plane as it went down.

"Yeah, we took shelter in a cave and saw the whole thing from there," Nancy told him. "Coach sent the four of us—me, George, Johnny, and Pete—out to see if anyone needed rescuing."

"Joe and I found the pilot," Frank explained. "He seems okay but a little confused."

He raked a hand through his hair. "We've got to get him to a doctor. We'll come back as fast as we can, but I figure it'll take two days to get to town and back. Will you be okay?"

"Things are heating up back at camp, but I think we can handle it."

"Nancy!" George's voice floated to their ears. "Where are you?"

"I'd better get going," Nancy whispered. "See you soon, Frank. Hurry back."

"We will," he promised, his brown eyes serious. "And, Nancy—be careful."

"What do you mean, no one was there?" Coach Pemberton demanded. "How could someone just get up and walk away from a plane crash?"

"I don't know, but he was gone, Coach," Johnny said, spreading his hands. "Maybe the pilot bailed out before the crash."

Nancy checked her watch. Eight o'clock. She, George, Johnny, and Pete had just returned from the crash site. Coach had come to the edge of the clearing outside the cave to meet them. Now he was furiously pacing back and forth.

Just beyond him Nancy saw that the rest of the group had set up camp for the night, their tents forming a loose ring just outside the cave where they had taken shelter earlier. The rain had stopped, but there wasn't enough dry wood for a fire to cook or ward off the cold.

The other group members were scattered around the clearing eating what looked like dried meat, nuts, and canned vegetables. Seeing heavy sweaters peeking out from under their ponchos, Nancy realized how cold she was, even in a thick long-sleeved knit shirt. But before she could change, she had to finish up with Coach Pemberton.

"Coach?" she said, turning back to him. He paused to look at her. "We should probably radio the authorities to report the crash."

Pemberton's face reddened, and his steel gray eyes bored into her as he sputtered, "We don't do anything until we find him—" Then he abruptly snapped his mouth shut and continued pacing.

"He seems awfully upset about that pilot's disappearance," George murmured to Nancy.

"Hey, Alvarez! Get out of my face, man!" Curt exclaimed suddenly.

Nancy watched as Curt pushed Johnny away from the rock he was sitting on. The rest of the group was clustered nearby, apparently listening to what Nancy had to report. "You're getting water all over me," he complained.

Johnny's poncho was still dripping from their trip through the soaked woods. "What's the big deal?" he asked Curt, obviously annoyed. "We've *all* been drenched today. What makes you so special?"

"Me?" Curt yelled. "Oh, that's funny, coming from Mr. Moody here. You're really beginning to bug me, you know?"

"He can't talk to you like that, Johnny!" Melissa cried. "Do something!"

Johnny and Curt were glaring at each other, fists clenching and unclenching. "Cut it out!" Coach Pemberton said sharply. He stepped up to the boys and, putting his hands on his hips, launched into a long lecture on teamwork and spirit. Johnny and Curt both interrupted with loud shouts at each other, which the coach responded to with more lecturing. "You guys aren't moving an inch until this is straightened out!" he yelled.

As the angry voices started up once again, Nancy realized that everyone's attention was focused on the argument. The tents were on the far side of the clearing, which was deserted. This was an opportunity she couldn't pass up, though it would be risky. She walked casually over to her pack, then edged toward Coach Pemberton's tent and ducked inside. It was definitely time to find out more about their group leader.

The first thing Nancy's eyes lit on was a compact, professional-looking short-wave radio. That's odd, she thought. There didn't seem to be a microphone.

On the far side of his sleeping bag was a clipboard and a small notebook with a black-and-white-marbled cover. Nancy opened it. The front page was divided into five columns.

The first was filled with names. "Osmian, Osmian, Jones, Osmian, Barnett," Nancy read.

The second column was a list of dates, and the third a list of numbers between one and fifteen. The fourth listed names of sports teams. Some of them Nancy recognized as major league clubs, but most of them she'd never heard of. One name, though, leapt out at her. *Briarcliff.*

The last column listed dollar amounts—mostly in the thousands.

Nancy sat back on her heels, her mind racing. Those numbers in the second column looked like point spreads—they were used for betting in football pools, to show the number of points by which a team had to win or lose in order to win the bet. And the dollar amounts in the last column must represent the amount of the bets. Nancy let out a low whistle.

Coach Pemberton was a serious gambler!

Chapter

Nine

C OME ON, Sleeping Beauty, keep your eyes open," Joe coaxed. He slapped the pilot's cheeks lightly. It was possible, though unlikely, that the man had a concussion. If so, sleep would be bad for him.

The man's pale blue eyes opened and focused on Joe. He seemed a bit more alert than before, but his gaze was still suspicious.

Joe sat down next to the man and leaned his back against the damp, mossy rock. What was taking Frank so long? Waiting in the persistent drizzle, Joe was beginning to feel cold and uncomfortable.

He shifted his eyes sideways to take in the pilot. Might as well try to find out a little about the guy. "I'm Joe Hardy," he said. "What's your name?"

Without turning his head, the pilot slid him a long look from those pale eyes. "Bill."

"Just plain Bill? Not Bill Smith? Or Bill Jones?" Joe pressed.

The pilot's head snapped toward Joe, and his mouth twisted into a sneering grimace. In a flash his meaty fist swung up and caught Joe on the side of the head.

"Hey!" Joe gasped. By snapping his head to the side he was able to lessen some of the blow's impact. Still, it made his ears ring.

The pilot jumped up and raced through the woods toward the crash site. "Stop!" Joe called, but the man didn't even slow down.

Shaking his head to clear the ringing, Joe got to his feet and started running after the man.

"What does this idiot think he's doing?" he muttered to himself. Joe played football for his high school team, and he considered himself to be in pretty good shape, but his muscles ached from the day's strenuous climbing. The pilot got a good lead on him.

Joe let out a sigh of relief when he saw his brother's blue poncho beyond the pilot. Frank was coming toward them through the trees.

"Grab him, Frank!" Joe yelled.

Frank dashed forward, his poncho a blue blur as he tackled the pilot around the waist. By the time Joe reached them, Frank had wrestled the heavy man to the ground and had pinned his arms firmly behind his back.

"What are you two doing?" Frank asked dryly, staring up at his brother. "Playing tag?"

Joe shook his head, panting. "The guy got spooked all of a sudden. Socked me in the head and took off."

Frank gazed down at the pilot, who was lying still, his eyes flitting between Joe and him. "Where were you trying to go?" Frank asked.

The pilot's lips thinned, and he began to curse the Hardys, struggling so desperately that finally Frank had to hold his legs while Joe sat on his chest.

"I'll tell you one thing," Joe grunted when they'd finally subdued the pilot. "This is not a seriously injured man. He's as strong as an ox!"

Frank shook his head. "We can't tell that for sure. We should still go through with our plan."

"Did you find Nancy?"

Frank nodded. "Yeah. Some other people from the group were with her, so we couldn't talk for long. I didn't get any details from her, but she says things are starting to happen in her group. We need to get our friend here"—he jerked his head at the pilot—"squared away in a hurry."

"Okay." Joe climbed to his feet and hauled the pilot up by one arm. The man seemed dazed and docile after his struggle, but Joe didn't trust him. "Let's go, Bill," he said. "And no tricks."

He and Frank led the pilot back to the moss-covered boulder where the backpacks were. Frank pulled a map of the area out of his pack and pored over it for a few minutes.

"It may save time if we head due west, rather than going back the way we came," he said at length. "See, there's a town on the other side of the range."

"Whatever you say, big brother," Joe replied, glancing at the spot Frank pointed to. He hoisted his backpack onto his back, adjusted the straps over his shoulders, and cinched the belt. "Let's hit the road."

Joe and Frank each took one of the pilot's arms again, and they set off. Bill stumbled between them without saying a word. All the fight seemed to have drained out of him.

The rain had stopped, but the sky remained overcast. As the day moved toward its close, the light among the tall evergreens grew dimmer and the air became cooler. In contrast to the rocky slope they'd negotiated earlier, this area was thickly wooded with evergreens and aspen.

"Ow!" Joe muttered as he stumbled over a protruding root. He straightened up again, only to crack his head sharply against the bough of a tree. "I wish we could trust you, Bill," he muttered. "Walking side by side like this is really slowing us down."

"Maybe we should rest," Frank suggested. "We probably shouldn't push Bill so hard, after that crash."

Joe shook his head. "Let's keep going for a while longer. We're going to have to stop soon anyway, before the sun sets," he argued. "With all these rain clouds, we won't have any moon or stars to help us out tonight."

"Let me rest," Bill said in a clear voice. "I'm worn out."

It was the first time he'd spoken since they'd started walking. Joe raised his eyebrows in surprise at the pilot's lucid tone. "Sounds as if his mind is unscrambling itself," he whispered to Frank as they spread out a tarpaulin to sit on. "Maybe he doesn't need a doctor after all."

"Well, we're stuck with him, anyway," Frank whispered back. "We can't just leave him here in the middle of the mountain to fend for himself."

"Yeah, you're right," Joe agreed with a sigh.

Frank doled out some trail mix and dried fruit, and the three ate. Then they sat in silence for a while. The pilot stretched out on his back and closed his eyes.

For the first time all day Joe realized how uncomfortable he was. He was soaked with water and mud and getting colder by the minute. He got his sweatshirt from his pack and put it on, but that didn't stop the uncomfortable itching. *I'd do anything for a nice hot* shower, he thought longingly as he scratched at the crust of mud behind his right ear.

Suddenly he cocked his head. Was that the rushing of a stream he heard, off to the left? Feeling a fresh burst of energy, Joe got to his feet and grabbed his flashlight and canteen from his pack. "I'm going to explore a little. Hand me your canteen, Frank. I'll see if I can fill it."

"Don't go too far," Frank warned. "You could get lost."

"Hey, I never get lost!" Joe scoffed. "I was a better Boy Scout than you, Frank."

"In your dreams, Joe," Frank retorted.

Joe headed off into the trees to his left. The sound of water grew steadily louder, and soon he found himself standing on the bank of a rain-swollen stream. Ha! he thought triumphantly. Joe Hardy never gets lost!

Crouching on a rock, he plunged his hands into the icy water, then scrubbed at his face and hair. It did a lot to rinse off the mud, but after that heavy downpour, there was too much grit swirling around in the water to make it drinkable. They'd have to wait until the next day to fill their canteens.

After he'd gotten off as much of the itchy mud as he could, Joe turned back and started out for the spot where he'd left Frank and the pilot.

At least, he was moving to where he thought

he'd left them. "Did I pass this tree before?" he muttered as he skirted a huge, rotting, upended trunk. He wasn't sure.

Joe wandered on for another five minutes, but all the trees really started to look the same. And it was too late in the day to orient himself by the sun. He switched on his flashlight and shone it at the surrounding trees and rocks, but still he couldn't figure out which way he'd come from. Finally Joe had to admit it—he was lost.

Man, is Frank going to rib me over this, Joe thought ruefully.

Sighing, Joe raised his hands to his mouth to scream his brother's name, but he was cut short when Frank's urgent voice rang out loudly from somewhere behind him.

"Joe! Bill's escaped!"

"What!" Joe leapt into action, crashing through the trees in the direction of Frank's voice. A moment later he nearly collided with his older brother. "What happened?" Joe cried.

"He bolted again, just a minute ago," Frank growled, rubbing the back of his head. "But not before he nearly brained me with a rock."

Joe raked his hands through his hair in frustration. "This guy can't possibly be worth all the trouble he's giving us," he muttered.

"He's out of his mind. We can't leave him out here alone," Frank said. "Come on!"

They shouldered their backpacks and hurried in the direction that Frank thought the pilot had taken. The forest was almost completely dark now. Using his flashlight, Joe managed to avoid large trees and rocks, but branches kept swatting him in the face, and he felt as if every root were jumping up to trip him.

"I hear noise up ahead," Frank said after a few minutes. "Man, he's loud enough for half a dozen people."

"Let's get him," Joe said determinedly. He shifted slightly to the right, toward the sound of crashing branches. Seconds later he and Frank burst into a small clearing—and skidded to a halt.

Bill the pilot was lying facedown on the ground, his hands tied behind his back. Flanking him were two hefty men in plaid hunting jackets. Each carried a shotgun.

The shotguns were trained unwaveringly on Frank and Joe!

Chapter

Ten

T HE SOUNDS OF YELLING outside the coach's tent brought Nancy out of her thoughts. The coach could come in any second. *I'd better get out before I get caught.*

She quickly replaced the marbled notebook beside the coach's sleeping bag. Cautiously lifting the canvas flap of the small tent, she saw that the coast was clear and quickly slipped out. Then she sauntered nonchalantly back to where the rest of the group was. Apparently the coach hadn't had any luck getting the two guys to calm down. If anything, the standoff between Johnny and Curt was escalating.

"Coach tells us we all have to treat you with kid gloves!" Curt shouted at Johnny. "We all have to watch out for your delicate feelings and act like nothing's ever your fault, even when it is!"

"What are you talking about?" Johnny demanded fiercely.

"Dave Bartel nearly died because of you," Curt flung back. "And your own sister—"

"Walker! That's enough!" Coach barked.

Ignoring the coach, Curt leveled a finger at Johnny. "I think you *are* a jinx!"

Total silence fell over the group.

Johnny threw off his poncho in a furious gesture, and clenching his fists, he launched himself at Curt. Curt staggered back and fell under the impact. In an instant the two boys were on the ground, punching each other wildly.

"You stole her from me!" Curt shouted.

"She dumped you, man," Johnny panted. He rolled over and pinned Curt's shoulders to the ground. "It had nothing to do with me."

"Walker! Alvarez! Break it up!" bellowed Coach Pemberton. He grasped Johnny by the collar of his shirt and pulled him away from Curt. "All right, all you other kids, clear out!"

So that's why Curt and Johnny aren't friends anymore, Nancy realized. And that's why there's all that weird stuff between Curt and Melissa. Melissa used to be Curt's girlfriend, and she dumped him for Johnny!

Melissa lingered long enough to place a manicured hand briefly on Johnny's shoulder,

Nancy noticed. There was a gleam of triumph in the petite girl's eyes as she turned and walked away.

As the coach began to lecture Curt and Johnny once again, Nancy turned away. She saw George setting up her tent and went to join her. There was a firm set to George's jaw. It couldn't have been fun for her to see the guy she liked fighting over another girl, Nancy realized.

Keeping her voice light, Nancy said, "I guess I have to change my vote on Curt. He could be the one behind the attacks on Johnny."

George didn't seem to hear her. "I can't believe two great guys like Curt and Johnny could start hating each other over Melissa," she muttered as Nancy pulled her own tent from her backpack. "Why can't he—*they* see through her?"

"You really do like Johnny, don't you?" Nancy asked softly, facing George.

George flushed, and her gaze dropped to the ground. "Sure I like him," she said. "He turned out to be a pretty nice guy."

"You know that's not what I mean," Nancy pressed.

After a moment George answered Nancy, "Maybe I do like him—in the way you mean. But so what? It's pretty obvious where he stands. He's Melissa's boyfriend, and that's exactly the way he wants it."

Nancy thought back to the way Johnny had

stared at George that morning by the lake. "I'm not sure Johnny knows what he wants," she said thoughtfully. "But if he can figure it out, I bet you'll be in for a nice surprise."

A small smile curved the corners of George's mouth. "Thanks for the vote of confidence, Nan."

Nancy grinned back. "No problem. Now, help me with this tent—and lean in close while you do it. I've got something to tell you!"

Frank didn't like staring down the barrels of shotguns. But the two guys in hunting jackets didn't look as if they were ready to trade places with Joe and him.

Who were they? It wasn't hunting season, Frank knew, not in summer. So whoever they were, their purpose probably wasn't lawful.

"Excuse me," he said, smiling politely. "I think we took a wrong turn somewhere. If you gentlemen will excuse us, we'll take our friend and be on our way." He stepped toward the spot where the tied-up pilot lay on the ground.

The larger of the two gunmen, a guy with matted brown hair and dark eyes, jerked his gun upward warningly. Frank froze, then raised his hands and clasped them on top of his head.

"Who are your young friends, Bob?" the shorter gunman asked the pilot in a soft, oily voice.

Bob? Frank wondered. It seemed as if these

guys knew the pilot, but the pilot had told Joe his name was Bill. What was going on?

Frank cast a sideways glance at Joe. He was standing still, his hands hanging loosely at his sides. Frank could see a telltale muscle flexing in Joe's jaw, though. He was ready for action.

When the pilot didn't answer, the tall gunman kicked him in the side. "Mr. Callahan asked you a question," he growled.

"I don't know who they are," the pilot replied, groaning. "Just a couple of punks I ran into in the woods."

"Sure," Callahan, the shorter one, said. "Too bad for them, isn't it? 'Cause now we'll have to take care of them as well."

A block of ice settled in the pit of Frank's stomach. Whatever he and Joe had just stumbled into, it was bad.

Out of the corner of his eye Frank caught a flicker of motion from Joe. No! he wanted to shout. Joe's hotheadedness wasn't what would help them now.

The two gunmen had apparently noticed Joe's movement, too. Both shotguns immediately swung over to cover him.

"Hey, take it easy! Guns make me nervous," Joe protested in an easy voice. "I was just going to put my pack down. Do you mind? It's heavy."

Frank suppressed a grin. Good thinking, little brother. Keep distracting them.

Callahan stared at him for a moment. Then he nodded. "Go ahead. Just move slow."

As Joe shed his pack, he caught Frank's gaze and nodded almost imperceptibly. Frank got the message—be ready to grab any chance that arises.

Under the tall one's watchful eye, Frank, too, shrugged out of his backpack. Meanwhile, Callahan tucked his gun into the crook of his arm, pulled a walkie-talkie from inside his hunting jacket, and started fiddling with it.

"Yeah, give me the boss," he said when a voice crackled out of the little radio.

Boss? Frank thought. That sounds like mobster talk. Mobsters in the Wyoming Rockies?

A moment later the radio crackled again, and a different, deeper voice came on.

"Boss, this is Callahan. We got him." Callahan paused as the voice crackled a question. "Where? I don't know," he replied. "Looks like nowhere to me. He's with a couple of kids."

"Crackle . . . plane?" asked the voice.

"No, we haven't found it yet. But there are about fifty of us out here looking. Even if our pal Bob gives us trouble—and he won't— some of the other guys will find it."

"What . . . *crackle* . . . kids?"

"Don't worry about them. We're about to put them out of commission. Over and out."

Frank tensed. This was it!

Callahan and his tall friend were now black silhouettes against the darkening gray of the woods, while the pilot was barely visible on the ground. Any fight could get confusing, but maybe that could work to their advantage.

"Sorry, kids, nothing personal," Callahan said as he tucked the walkie-talkie back inside his jacket. "It's just business."

"Come on," Joe said amiably, stepping forward. "Surely there's no need for *violence!*"

On the last word his leg lashed up and out in a kick aimed at Callahan's gun hand. The mobster cried out as his weapon flew from his hand.

At the same time Frank launched himself at the big gangster's legs with a yell. Diving in low, he threw his full weight into the tackle. The man went down with a thud and lay there, momentarily stunned. Frank felt around until he found the guy's shotgun, then hurled it across the clearing.

"All right!" came Joe's triumphant voice.

Frank looked up, breathing hard. His brother was cradling Callahan's shotgun in the crook of his elbow. It was trained on the gangsters. "Now, boys, no sudden moves," he said, grinning so that his teeth shone in the darkness. "Like I said, guns make me nervous."

"Don't listen to him. He's a crack shot," Frank advised the two men. He dug into his backpack for rope to tie them up.

When he was done, Frank turned to the pilot. "Let's go, Bill or Bob or whatever your name is," he said. He unhooked his Swiss army knife from his belt and cut the pilot's bonds. Then he, Joe, and the pilot turned to go.

"You won't get away with this," Callahan called after them. "This whole area is crawling with men. And when they find you, they won't be as nice as we were!"

"We'll risk it, thanks," Joe called over his shoulder. But when they were out of the clearing, Frank could see that his brother's expression was anxious. "The guy's right," Joe said, reading Frank's mind. "What are we going to do?"

Frank had been turning over the options in his head, and they weren't ideal. "We have only one choice," he said at last. "We can't go down, because that's where the bad guys are. So we'll have to go up—and we'll have to travel tonight. Our best chance is to hook up with Nancy and George's group. They may have a radio transmitter we can use to call the police."

"Let's move, then," Joe said. "You tie good knots, but they won't hold those two forever."

Frank nodded. Sooner or later the other

mobsters would find out that their quarry had escaped.

If they manage to catch up to Joe and me before we make it down the mountain, Frank told himself, those crooks will make sure we never see civilization again.

Chapter

Eleven

W ELL, AT LEAST it's a nice day," Pete Shimoya said. He finished knotting his bandanna around his forehead and looked up at the sky.

"Clear and warm," Nancy agreed. It was about seven o'clock, and traces of early mist still drifted up from the grass. "Hey, don't look so gloomy, Pete. We'll have a great time today!"

Pete's expression was skeptical. "Is that a promise or just a hope?" he asked her. "The team feeling in this group stinks."

Nancy had to agree. The group was more divided than ever. Not to mention that Pemberton had a serious gambling habit—though Nancy wasn't sure how, or even if, that fit into everything else. And now, if there were any more attacks, the Hardys wouldn't be around to help.

Nonetheless, Nancy was feeling hopeful—maybe it was the gorgeous weather. She pulled her hair back into a ponytail and clasped it with a barrette.

She turned as George came up, her arms cradling their sleeping bags. "Let's spread these out to dry some before we take off," George suggested.

"Good idea," Nancy replied. The two girls headed for a big, flat-topped boulder a few hundred feet from the camp.

George touched Nancy's arm and held a finger to her lips, then pointed toward a reed-fringed stream that wound nearby.

When Nancy looked, her lips parted in wonder. A female elk and her calf had come to the water's edge to drink. The mother stood watchfully, her head turning slowly from side to side as she checked for signs of danger. The calf, no more than a few months old, had wide, innocent eyes. Its long legs splayed comically as it bent to the stream. It was adorable!

Nancy grabbed George's arm as something hit the water with a tremendous splash, right in front of the mother elk. The graceful animal reared back on its hind legs. In an instant she rounded up her calf and fled for the safety of the woods.

George let out a little cry of disappointment. "What happened?"

A moment later Nancy recognized Curt's tall figure emerging from a clump of reeds. As he walked toward Nancy and George, Nancy saw that a ferocious scowl wrinkled his brown skin, and his eyebrows were drawn together in a V.

George put her hands on her hips. "What's the big idea?" she demanded angrily.

"George, don't push," Nancy murmured. Curt looked as if he was in a foul temper. "Hi, Curt," she greeted him in a friendly tone.

"Uh, hey," he mumbled, his expression softening. "Sorry. I guess I was just taking out some bad feelings. I threw a rock and it landed in the stream. I didn't mean to scare the elk."

Nancy shrugged. "Understandable," she said. "There seems to be enough of it going around."

"No kidding," Curt said with a sour smile. Sitting down, Nancy leaned back on the sun-warmed rock. It seemed as good a time as any to get to the bottom of what was going on among the Briarcliff students. Taking a deep breath, she said to Curt, "Can I ask you something? What made you and Melissa break up?"

Curt's frown reappeared. He hesitated for a moment, staring at Nancy, then said slowly, "Everything was fine when Alvarez and I were both second-string players. But last year Johnny got to be Mr. Big Shot Quarterback, and then he moved in on Melissa."

"Moved in?" Nancy repeated. "How?"

"I don't know—he must have done it behind my back," Curt said, anger creeping back into his voice. "All I know is, one day she was mine forever, and the next she was telling me to take a hike. A couple of months later she started turning up everywhere with *him*." There was a short pause before he sneered, "My best friend."

"It seems a little unfair to blame the whole thing on Johnny," George commented.

Curt swung around on her. "I guess I'm just wasting time talking to you two," he said furiously. "You're already on Alvarez's side."

"Wait, Curt—"

But he interrupted Nancy. "You'd better be careful. Haven't you figured out yet that it's not healthy to be friends with that guy?"

With that he walked away. George drew in a breath. "Whoa," she said. "Was that a threat?"

"I'm not sure," answered Nancy. "Maybe he was just referring to the claim that Johnny's a jinx. Let's keep an eye on him, though. No point in taking chances."

When they returned to the campsite, Johnny and Stasia were serving up hot breakfast cereal from a pot over the fire. Melissa sat to the side, putting a coat of clear polish on her nails. Both

Curt and Johnny seemed tense and moody as they all ate. Coach, too, seemed on edge. He kept pacing to the edge of the campsite, peering out over the valley below. It was almost as if he expected to see something specific, Nancy mused.

"Okay!" he called suddenly, moving into the center of the campsite. "We're wasting time. Let's clean up, get packed, and hit the trail."

Nancy and George were on cleanup duty, so they carried all the dishes to the stream and rinsed them. Then they collected their bedding from the rock and went back to the campsite. Nancy was surprised to see that their tents had already been taken down and stowed in their packs, along with their gear.

"We all pitched in," Johnny explained in response to her questioning look. "Coach is in a hurry to get going."

Nancy and George distributed the aluminum dishes, then shouldered their packs. "Melissa must have packed mine," Nancy joked to George. "It feels twice as heavy as it did yesterday."

Finally they set off. Coach seemed eager to make up the miles they'd lost the previous day. He set a fast pace. "I hope the Hardys will be able to find us again," Nancy whispered to George. "At this rate we could be in Canada by nightfall!"

* * *

"Coach, I can't take any more. Isn't it time for lunch yet?" Breathless, Curt flung himself down to rest at the foot of a cliff that was about a dozen feet high.

"It must be," panted George, wiping her brow with the back of her hand. "This rock climbing is murder!"

Nancy was about to flop down next to George when the coach grinned, saying, "Not quite. Next comes a lesson in knots and rope handling."

They had just spent two hours practicing rock-climbing techniques. Coach Pemberton had shown them how to plan out a good climbing route, how to pick crevices for hand- or footholds, and how to cling to overhangs. Then they had taken turns scrambling up and down the twelve-foot cliff.

It had taken a lot of concentration to get the hang of it. They had all been working so hard to improve their technique, Nancy noticed, that the bickering had pretty much stopped.

Once again she found herself impressed with Coach Pemberton's knowledge and teaching skills. She still didn't trust him, but he certainly was good at his job! Everyone seemed to enjoy the lesson as much as she did—or almost everyone.

"Knots!" Melissa muttered in a disgusted tone. She gazed at her hands. "My nails are already totally mangled."

George rolled her eyes at Nancy but didn't say anything.

The knots lesson took another hour. The coach made them practice bowlines, figure eights, butterfly knots, and sheet bends until they could do them without thinking about the moves.

As Nancy worked with her rope, she kept smelling a faint but familiar chemical odor. What is it? she asked herself, wrinkling her nose. She couldn't quite place it.

"Okay!" said the coach, clapping his hands. "That's enough knots. Now show me who can make it to the top of the practice cliff fastest. On your marks, get set—go!"

Melissa and Stasia stayed put, but Nancy, George, and all four boys threw down their ropes and raced for the cliff. Nancy scrambled up as fast as she could, but one person beat her.

"I made it!" Johnny cried, standing on top of the cliff. He was flushed and smiling. When Nancy pulled herself up and saw the glow in his green eyes, she didn't mind a bit that he'd beaten her. George and Dan reached the top a moment later, with Pete and Curt not far behind.

"Good going, Alvarez," Coach Pemberton called up heartily.

Looking down, Nancy saw Melissa glaring up at Johnny. What's she so mad about? Then

Nancy noticed that Johnny kept stealing glances at George.

Finally, at the coach's urging, the six racers made their way back down the cliff. After picking up their ropes, the group set off again.

Their route led them along a line of granite outcroppings that grew ever higher. Soon they were hiking single file along a strip that was only about six feet wide. The rock dropped off to the right in a huge crevasse that separated the mountain they were on from another, higher peak.

Then Curt, who was in the lead, stopped. "Hey, Coach," he said, "our path just ended. Do we have to jump across the gorge, or what?"

"You could try," Pemberton replied, chuckling. "But, in fact, there's a path." He made his way to the front of the group and pointed to a narrow, uneven shelf that ran along the cliff. It was littered with shale and loose debris.

Curt's jaw dropped. "We have to cross *that*? It can't be more than two feet wide."

"That's right. Here's a chance to practice your bowlines," Coach said. "We're going to rope ourselves together. If one of us slips, the rest will anchor that person so he doesn't fall into the crevasse. I'd better go first."

"Coach, let me," Johnny put in suddenly.

Pemberton hesitated, but he looked pleased. "All right," he said. "Drew, you go second.

Pete Shimoya third, Fayne fourth, Walker fifth, Somers sixth, Dan Shimoya seventh, Kominsky eighth. I'll bring up the rear."

When they were all roped together, the coach showed them how to make sliding anchors by looping their lines around any protrusions in the cliff wall. That way the group would always be attached to the rocks at one or two points.

Finally Johnny started cautiously along the ledge, Nancy right behind him. "It's slippery," he called back. "Be careful, everyone."

Inch by inch they made their way across the narrow, treacherous shelf. Nancy flattened herself against the rock face with her hands spread out. When they were almost across, she glanced over her shoulder down into the crevasse. Her heart jumped into her throat. It was a long way down!

Just then Nancy felt a tug on the rope that attached her to Johnny. "Whoa!" she heard him gasp.

A quick glimpse told Nancy he'd lost his footing. There was a loud clattering as bits of shale bounced into the crevasse. He was teetering, and Nancy had to fight to keep her own balance.

"Johnny—look out!"

In trying to regain his footing, he had swung too far to the left. Nancy's heart pounded as he pitched forward into the crevasse!

The anchoring rope, she remembered. It will hold him. But no sooner did the thought cross her mind than his anchor rope snapped!

Nancy didn't even stop to think. She just reached out and snatched the frayed end of Johnny's rope, wrapping it once around her hand.

The next thing she knew, Johnny's weight was pulling her over the edge with him!

Chapter
Twelve

NANCY SCREAMED as she felt herself plunging headfirst over the ledge. Her screaming was abruptly cut short, though, by a sharp blow to her solar plexus. It was her safety rope, she realized—it had held. An instant later she felt a sharp pull on the rope in her hand as Johnny jerked to a halt below her. She moved her left hand down and clutched his safety rope as tightly as she could with two hands now.

Above her she could hear a babble of voices.

"Help!" she cried.

"Hang on, Nan! Hang on, Johnny!" George's voice called. "We won't let you go."

Nancy dangled helplessly in midair, her entire attention focused on not letting the rope in her hands go. But Johnny was so heavy—she didn't know how much longer she could hold him!

Just then she felt the strain ease up. Glancing downward, Nancy saw that Johnny had worked his way over and was clinging desperately to the cliff face. His eyes were shut tight, his face contorted with the effort. He had wedged one foot into a crack in the granite, and both hands were gripping a slight protrusion above his head.

With a sigh of relief Nancy quickly adjusted her grip on his safety rope, wrapping it around both hands now to make it more secure. But she knew that if Johnny lost his hold on the cliff face, she wouldn't be able to support his weight for more than a minute or so.

"What should we do?" Nancy recognized Pete Shimoya's voice. He had been right behind her in line, she remembered.

"What's happening?" came Coach Pemberton's deep voice from the rear of the line. "I can't see anything! What's going on?"

Oh, no! Nancy thought. He's panicking, and no one else knows what to do!

Then George's voice rang out firmly. "Everybody, find something to anchor yourselves to," she called to the others. "We're going to haul Nancy and Johnny up, and we'll need as many free hands as we can get."

"All right, George!" Nancy cheered weakly.

"Nancy, Johnny, can you get rid of your

packs?" Pete asked. "It'll be easier to haul you up without the extra weight."

"I can't," said Johnny in a high, panicked voice. "I'm barely holding on as it is!"

Pete's calming voice immediately answered him, "Don't worry about it, Johnny. How about you, Nancy? Can you dump yours?"

Nancy wasn't sure how she did it, but she unfastened the buckle of the waist strap by hitting the clicker with her elbow. She slid one arm free by carefully shifting Johnny's rope to her other hand. Then she reversed the process and shrugged the pack off her other side. She gulped as she watched it hurtle into the depths of the crevasse.

A second later the rope around her waist tightened, and she felt herself being pulled slowly upward.

"Okay, Johnny!" Nancy shouted to him. "Let go of the rock, but gently. Try not to swing."

"Okay," he gasped in a voice filled with terror.

A moment later his safety rope went taut in her hands again. Nancy winced and tried not to cry out as the nylon dug into her flesh. Then, abruptly, she was sliding over the edge of the shelf to safety. Two pairs of hands reached down and started hauling in Johnny's rope. When she saw that Pete and George had a firm hold, Nancy released the rope and leaned back against the cliff face.

Soon Johnny's head appeared over the ledge, followed by his torso. He crawled onto the shelf next to Nancy. Then the two of them crawled the rest of the way across the ledge, to the open rocky area on the other side. Once there Nancy threw herself down on the ground and just lay there for a minute. Johnny flopped down next to her.

"Nan, are you okay?" George asked anxiously. "Did you hurt yourself?"

"Nothing major." Nancy looked at her rope-burned hands, then gazed up at George. "You saved our lives," she said softly. "Thanks!"

"Hey, how many times have *you* rescued *me?*" George asked lightly, but Nancy saw tears shining in her friend's big brown eyes.

Nancy raised her head as Coach Pemberton came over to them, his face white. "How did it happen?" he asked.

Johnny held up the end of his safety rope for the coach to see. Pemberton's eyes went wide as he inspected it. He seemed genuinely surprised and more than a little upset.

"But all our ropes are brand-new!" Pemberton sputtered. "How could it snap like that?"

Nancy thought she had a pretty good idea. "Let's see that rope," she said, holding out her hand. She took the frayed end and peered at it. Some of the broken fibers were a little less frayed than the others, but she couldn't say for sure that the rope had been cut. Still, she was almost certain that that was what had happened.

Nancy was about to hand the rope back to Johnny when she was struck by the same faint chemical odor she'd smelled earlier when they were practicing knots. She sniffed the rope again but couldn't identify the scent. Maybe it was something they used in making the ropes.

Coach Pemberton's deep voice drew Nancy away from her thoughts. "Well, I'll complain to the manufacturers when we get back," the coach was saying. "Meanwhile, we'd better get back to business." He straightened and called out, "Who are our lunch cooks today?"

George and Dan raised their hands.

"Okay, everyone, let's see your food stores," said Dan, loosening the flap of his backpack. "George and I will come up with an amazing concoction for your dining pleasure."

But when everyone had produced the food they had in their packs, the pile was surprisingly small. George stared at it in dismay. "What happened to all our provisions?" she asked. "This doesn't look like enough to last us through tomorrow."

Nancy drew in her breath, then said slowly, "My pack was really heavy. I think maybe it had most of the food in it. Whoever packed it this morning must have just tossed in any food that was lying around."

She shifted her gaze to Melissa, but the dark-haired girl studiously avoided her gaze.

"Your pack's down at the bottom of that crevasse," Dan pointed out, frowning. "And that means we're out of food."

"Who packed Drew's backpack?" Coach demanded, facing each member of the group in turn.

"I did," Melissa admitted reluctantly. "I guess I didn't realize I was putting so much stuff in it."

Coach opened his mouth to say something but stopped himself as Curt muttered something under his breath. "What was that, Walker?" the coach asked, swinging around sharply.

Curt seemed momentarily embarrassed. Then defiance came into his dark eyes. "I said, what's the point of trying to blame someone? We all know what the real problem is."

"Oh? What's that?" Coach asked. His voice was calm, but Nancy saw his face redden.

"It's our jinx," Curt replied in a firm voice, nodding his head toward Johnny.

"It's kind of like this trip is cursed," Stasia piped up. Her voice became upbeat as she added, "Maybe we should turn back."

Coach Pemberton shook his head in disgust. "Turn back! Forget it. Just because we don't have ready-made rations doesn't mean we have to go hungry. There's food here, if you know how to find it—and I do."

Johnny had been silent, but now he spoke up. "They're right." He stood up and moved away, hands in his pockets.

Coach Pemberton stared at Johnny's back for a moment. Then, shaking his head in disgust, he stalked over to his pack, pulled the topographical map from the top flap, and began to study it.

As George started collecting twigs from the surrounding wooded area, Nancy glanced over to where Johnny was standing. He was staring out over the wide crevasse they'd just escaped, a defeated expression on his face.

Nancy made up her mind then and there. It was time to tell Johnny the truth. She couldn't just let him keep thinking he was a jinx—not when she had proof that he was the victim of sabotage.

"That's impossible!" Johnny exclaimed, shaking his head adamantly. "None of my friends would want to hurt me."

"Are you sure?" Nancy asked gently. "Are you really sure Curt's still your friend?"

Johnny remained firm. "He's not that kind of guy," he insisted. "Sure, he might pick a fight with me, but he'd never do anything behind my back."

"Well, *someone* is sabotaging your equipment." She started to repeat what she'd already told him about the carabiner hooks and the rope, but he held up his hand to silence her.

"I'm not going to listen to that kind of talk about my friends. That's final." With that he turned from the ledge and went to join Melissa and Stasia.

Sighing, Nancy watched him go. She just hoped he came to his senses before someone put him out of commission—for good.

"This is hopeless," Pete Shimoya announced. "The fish know I'm here. They're hiding from me."

Nancy finished applying salve to the rope burns on her hands and looked over to see Pete throw his makeshift spear aside and splash out of the stream. He sat down on the rocky bank and wiped his forehead with his bandanna.

It was about seven o'clock, and the group had set up camp for the night in a field with a stream running through it. Coach had halted early that day, so that he could give them a lesson on which plants were edible. He'd also made everyone sharpen a stick for spearing trout. Johnny, Curt, Melissa, Dan, and Stasia were all standing knee-deep in the stream, but so far no one had caught anything.

Curt put his spear aside, too, and climbed out of the shallow water. "I think I'll go and see if I can find any more of those edible mushrooms you showed us, Coach," he said pleasantly. "Maybe we'll have some tonight."

Nancy stared at him, suddenly suspicious. He'd been irritable all day; why did he sound so pleasant now? What was on his mind? She leaned over to George, who was piling wood up beside the spot where they would build their fire later.

"I'll be back," Nancy whispered. "If anyone asks where I am, make something up." Then she strolled casually after Curt.

He entered the forest. Nancy stayed about fifty feet behind him as he moved slowly, a cooking pot held loosely in one hand. He bent down every so often to examine things on the ground.

Am I being ridiculous? Nancy wondered as she crept from rock to rock. He's probably doing just what he said—searching for mushrooms.

Nancy ducked behind a tree as Curt paused and checked behind himself. It's a good thing this forest is evergreen, she thought. Pine needles don't make nearly as much noise as dead leaves when someone walks through them.

She was about to start forward again when she heard a faint rustling behind her. But before she could turn, Nancy felt something hard strike her sharply on the back of the head. Stars exploded in front of her eyes, and the woods narrowed into a shadowy tunnel.

Then blackness swept over everything.

Chapter

Thirteen

NANCY'S EYES fluttered open. The world swirled around her in a dark haze, and she blinked, trying to get her bearings. It was nighttime, she saw. The air on her bare arms was cold. Her cheek was resting against a bed of pine needles, and her head was pounding.

What happened? Where am I? She started to lift her head, but a throbbing pain shot through it. Then it all came back to her—how she'd been following Curt and was hit from behind. She held her watch up and the glow-in-the-dark hands told her it was after eight. She must have been unconscious for an hour.

Nancy sat up slowly, clutching at her aching head. Who hit me? she wondered. Curt didn't do it, because I was staring straight at him when it happened. So who was it? And why did the person knock me out?

She cocked her head to one side. What was that crashing noise? Had the coach sent someone out to look for her? That didn't make sense. They'd be calling her name.

There it was again, and it was loud. Nancy caught her breath as the noise moved closer. It sounded big—really big. She peered wildly into the darkness. A bear?

Suddenly a gigantic form erupted from the shadows—and it moved right toward her!

"Nancy!" an astonished male voice cried.

Nancy blinked, unable to believe her ears. "Joe?" she said shakily.

The dark form had stopped, and Nancy heard the sound of fumbling in the dark. Then a flashlight clicked on, blinding her. Squinting, she put up a hand to shield her eyes. The light was shifted, and now Nancy could just make out the faces of the Hardys. With them was a third man, a heavy, middle-aged guy who seemed to be wearing hiking clothes also. She didn't recognize him, though.

"Nancy, what are you doing out here?" Frank asked. He came over to her, and she could see the concern on his face as he helped her to her feet. "Are you hurt? Wow, your skin is like ice. Let me get you a shirt."

She smiled gratefully as he handed her a flannel shirt, which she put on over her T-shirt. "Someone KO'ed me from behind," she explained, gingerly massaging the back of her head, where a big lump had formed. "What are *you* guys doing here?"

Frank and Joe looked at each other. Then Joe put a hand on the third guy's shoulder and pushed him forward. "Meet Bill," he said to Nancy.

As she gazed at the older man again, Nancy's mind began to clear more. "The pilot of the plane that went down last night?" she guessed.

Frank nodded. "Joe and I were taking him to a town where he could get some medical help," he explained. "The thing is, along the way we ran into some resistance, in the form of two mobsters."

"Mobsters?" Nancy echoed dubiously. "In the Rockies? Frank, are you sure?"

"I know it sounds weird," he told her. "But it's true. We heard them talking to some of their, uh, colleagues, and it definitely sounded like mob talk to us."

"But what are they doing here?" Nancy wanted to know. "What are they after?"

"That's the thing we don't really get," Joe replied. "They seem to be after our pal Bill. Only they keep calling him Bob, and he swears he doesn't know who they are or what they want—"

"I don't!" the pilot broke in. "I told you,

they must have mistaken me for someone else. I don't know anything about any mob."

The guy's voice had an edge to it that Nancy didn't trust. She had a feeling he was lying, but that didn't change the fact that mobsters were after him—and anyone who was with him.

"Anyway," Frank went on in an urgent voice, "before we got away from the two guys I mentioned, we found out that this area is crawling with thugs, all looking for our guy here. Bill or Bob or whoever."

"They're working their way up the mountains. Some of them may be coming this way soon," Joe added, his blue eyes deadly serious. "And let me tell you, if they're half as nasty as the two we met, you don't want to run into them."

Nancy let out a long breath. "This day has been too much," she said, groaning. "First I nearly plunge to my doom in a ravine, then somebody sneaks up behind me and bashes me on the head, and now you guys show up to tell me we're surrounded by an army of mobsters!"

A determined expression lit up her face as she added, "We'd better come up with a plan. What do you think we should do?"

She could see Frank's teeth extra white as he grinned at her in the darkness. "All right! That sounds like the Nancy Drew I know!

"The main thing is," he went on, "I think

it's time for Joe and me to show ourselves. I mean, whatever shenanigans are going on in your group, at least none of those people are professional criminals."

"As far as we know," Nancy told him. "I did find out that Coach Pemberton's a pretty heavy gambler—though so far there doesn't seem to be any connection between that and the attacks."

The pilot twitched and seemed about to say something, but when they all turned to him, he shook his head. "It's nothing," he said.

Joe picked up the conversation. "The mobsters are our biggest danger now. We're going to have to work together if we want to get off these mountains alive."

Nancy thought it over for a minute, then nodded. "You're right. But how can we explain you guys to everyone else?"

"Let's tell the truth, as much as we can," Frank suggested. "We don't have to say anything about *why* we're here. I doubt anyone'll ask, anyway."

"Sounds good. Let's go." Taking the flashlight from Frank, Nancy shone it around to get her bearings. She still felt a little lightheaded, but she was steady enough to lead the way back to the campsite. As they walked, she brought the Hardys up to date on what had happened that day, including Curt's threat, the cut rope, and how she had followed Curt that evening.

"But he wasn't the one who hit me," she

concluded. "Someone else is getting nervous about my poking around. The question is, who?"

When they arrived at the campsite, Nancy spotted Coach's form beside the fire. He was bent over a map and seemed to be making notations on it. The others were in small groups, talking.

"Nan, you're back!" George called as Nancy stepped out of the shadows. "I was just about to—" George broke off when she spotted Frank and Joe. As surprised as she must have been, she controlled herself and didn't say anything more.

Taking a deep breath, Nancy led the Hardys and the pilot past George and the other members of the group. Coach Pemberton didn't even glance up from his map when she approached the fire.

"Back so soon, Drew?" he said coolly. "Well, you managed to skip cooking, but there's still plenty of cleanup left. . . ." He raised his head then and saw the three guys with Nancy, and his speech trailed off, his mouth wide open.

Nancy jumped in before he could recover. "Coach, I ran into these guys in the woods," she said briskly. "They have something very important to tell us. It concerns us all." She took in each face in the circle. Curt was with them, she noted. On the ground next to him was a cooking pot full of mushrooms.

"What news?" the coach demanded, his gaze riveted on the pilot, Frank, and Joe. "What are you talking about?"

Swiftly Frank and Joe told Coach Pemberton and the others about the mobsters.

When the Hardys were done, the coach said with what he thought was a tolerant smile, "This is all very amusing, but surely you don't expect us to believe it?"

Nancy glanced at everyone else. They were all staring at the Hardys with expressions of fear and amazement. Clearly they all believed the Hardys' story. Why was Coach Pemberton so skeptical?

"You say these fellows you ran into were wearing hunting jackets?" Coach went on. He waved his hand around at the group. "Seems to me those fellows were simply poachers. There's a lot of big game in these parts, you know."

Frank folded his arms, and Nancy could tell he was getting impatient. "Maybe so," he said evenly, "but how many poachers do you know who hunt humans and use walkie-talkies to talk to their bosses?"

Coach Pemberton let out a guffaw. "I think they were just trying to scare you kids with all that nonsense," he said. "They didn't want you going back and telling the rangers about them, so they pretended they were real bad guys." Turning to the pilot, he said, "You were there. Did those men strike you as dangerous criminals?"

The pilot shrugged beneath his green plaid shirt. His eyes roved nervously around the campsite. "They just looked like hunters to me."

The coach turned triumphantly to Nancy. "You see?"

Nancy stared at the pilot, bewildered. Why had he sided with the coach? He *had* claimed before that he didn't know what the mobsters wanted, but at least he'd sounded as if he believed they were real. Had that been Nancy's imagination? Or was the pilot playing some game of his own?

"Look," said Joe, stepping forward. "You don't know who we are, and it's your choice to believe us or not. But my brother and I aren't just a couple of wild kids. We've had experience dealing with criminals. These guys are nothing to joke about. They're all over this area, and if you run into them you'll be in for rough times."

"Coach," Johnny called hesitantly from where he was sitting on a sleeping bag, "what if these guys are right? I mean, their story sounds pretty convincing to me."

All right, Johnny! Nancy felt like applauding him for taking a stand.

"I agree with Johnny," Stasia joined in.

Nancy looked expectantly at Dan and Pete,

who'd been talking quietly. "So do we," said Dan. "Maybe we should think about cutting this trip short—as of right now."

"What?" Coach barked. His nostrils flared. "Absolutely not. There is no reason whatsoever to interrupt our expedition. End of discussion." Turning on his heel, he strode to his tent and disappeared inside.

A buzz of conversation began. "We have to do something," George said firmly. "It's obvious Coach Pemberton isn't going to. I say we borrow his shortwave radio and contact the state police."

Nancy had been about to suggest that herself. Shooting her friend a grin, she said, "Come on, let's ask now."

"I'll be right back," Joe said quietly to Nancy. "I just want to check something out."

Nancy gave him a distracted nod, then led the others to the coach's tent. When she called his name, Coach Pemberton stuck his head out through the flap. "What is it now?" he asked, glaring at them.

It was Frank who replied. "We understand you have a radio. May we borrow it? We'd like to tell our story to the police and see what they think."

A curious gleam came into Coach Pemberton's gray eyes. "Funny you should ask," he drawled. "Because when I came in here, look what I found." He reached behind him and pulled out a mangled object, which he held up for everyone to see.

Nancy gasped. The radio was smashed to bits!

"Who could have done this?" the coach asked softly.

No one answered, but Nancy thought of someone immediately—someone who had motive *and* opportunity to break the radio: Coach Pemberton.

For the second time Nancy noticed that the console had no microphone. Until now she had assumed the coach simply hadn't hooked up the microphone. Now she wondered if he hadn't brought one. The coach could have deliberately smashed the radio so that the others wouldn't find out it couldn't be used to transmit, only to receive. Apparently he had never intended to use the radio for anything except listening to other frequencies. The question was, why was Coach trying to hide that fact?

When I find that out, Nancy thought, I may learn the answers to a whole lot of questions.

Chapter

Fourteen

FRANK STARED at Coach Pemberton in confusion. The guy didn't want to get them down off the mountain. It was almost as if he wanted to keep everyone up there and isolated.

At that moment Joe came running up and skidded to a stop next to Frank. "Bad news! I just climbed a tree to see if I could spot any movement. A bunch of lights are moving up the valley below us—twenty of them, at least, spread out in a loose chain. Looks like they're headed this way."

Beside Frank, the pilot drew in a sharp breath.

"Joe, how far away are they?" Nancy asked. "Could you tell?"

"My guess is that they'll be here in about a

half hour." Joe was shifting his weight from foot to foot, obviously anxious to get moving.

The group leader's steel gray eyes now showed alarm, Frank saw. "Now do you believe us?" Frank asked.

"Well, I—" Coach cleared his throat, then said stiffly, "I still don't believe your mobster story, but I can't imagine any good reason why people would be moving through these mountains at night."

"Neither can I," Joe burst out. "But I can think of plenty of nasty reasons. Come on, we can't stand here debating it all night. We have to get out of here before they find us!"

"Joe's right," Nancy said.

Coach Pemberton hesitated, and Frank thought he saw him dart a quick glance at the pilot, but he couldn't be sure. Finally the coach said, "Okay, let's break camp. Hop to it, folks!"

Finally! Tapping Joe on the shoulder, Frank said, "Let's douse that fire before someone sees it."

They all worked quickly. Frank could almost smell the fear in the air, but he was relieved that so far no one had panicked. Ten minutes later a silent group set off, heading up toward the mountain's peak.

The coach took the lead, so Frank decided to go last, where he could keep an eye peeled for anyone approaching their rear. It took only a few minutes for his eyes to adjust to the darkness, and a half-moon gave him some light.

He knew from their map that the mountain they were on was one of the lower ones in the Wind River range. Instead of being capped with bare granite and snowfields, it was forested most of the way up. At least they would have good cover while they traveled, and their feet made little more than a rustle on the soft pine needles covering the ground.

Still, Frank felt uneasy at the deadly game of hide-and-seek they were playing. As long as they were trapped in the mountains, they were at risk. If only there was some way to call for help. Hey, he thought suddenly. Maybe there *is* a way!

"I need to check out something at the crash site," he murmured to Joe, who was walking just in front of him.

Joe's voice was filled with doubt as he said, "The crash site? That must be over an hour's hike from here. Are you crazy?"

Ignoring his brother, Frank took off his pack and handed it to Joe. "Can you manage this? I'll catch up with you."

He slipped unobtrusively into the shadow from a big tree before Joe had time to object.

Frank winced as a branch snapped under his foot. He wasn't traveling as silently as he would have liked, but then, he was in a hurry. The faster he moved, the better his chances of beating the mobsters to the plane.

Frank needed to check out the plane's radio. Despite the fire, the control panel had been in fairly good condition, he thought from his brief glimpse of it. Joe had interrupted Frank's search of the plane's interior when he'd found the pilot. And Bill had been so disoriented that he'd had to leave without checking the plane out thoroughly. Maybe the radio was working, and he could use it to call for help.

He'd been heading steadily down and west for the past hour, every now and then climbing a tree to check his progress against the barrenness of the granite cliff where the plane had gone down. He knew he was close now. Just another couple of minutes and he'd be there. He hurried through a dense tangle of fallen branches.

"What—" Frank felt a jolt as he collided with another body!

The other guy let out a startled grunt, and Frank saw a beefy silhouette whip around to face him. Moonlight glinted on the barrel of an efficient-looking MAC-10 semiautomatic gun in the man's hands.

"Uh-oh," Frank muttered.

The man gave an ugly grin. "What have we here?" His voice rose a little as he called out, "Boys, I just caught a live one!"

Seconds later three more men materialized out of the darkness, all carrying shotguns. A feeling of dread knotted Frank's stomach.

One of the three newcomers, a big guy with dark, curly hair, peered at Frank and said, "He could be one of those punks that jumped Callahan and Lorenzo."

Frank gulped as the first guy he'd run into raised his gun to his shoulder. "I don't know who you are, but you're gonna tell us where our friend Bob is, and where his plane is. Because if you don't—"

At that moment a scream rang out from the woods to his left.

Frank didn't stop to wonder who it was. As the guy with the MAC-10 whipped his head around to look behind him, Frank lashed out with his foot, knocking the gun out of the man's hands. In another instant he'd seized it and had it aimed at the thug.

"Hey!" one of the other mobsters yelled. He sounded outraged.

"Back off," Frank ordered. He gestured with the MAC-10 at the three who still held shotguns. "And toss those things away!"

One by one the gangsters threw their weapons into the woods. Frank searched them for rope, but there was none. Nor did they have a walkie-talkie. *Now* what was he going to do? He couldn't sit around and baby-sit them all night. He had to get to the plane before more of their mobster buddies showed up.

"On your bellies," Frank commanded, thinking fast. "Faces to the ground. The last one down is the first one to get it. Now, move it!" He made his voice as menacing as possible, and the mobsters jumped to obey.

Frank took a deep breath. If this was going to work, they had to believe he meant business. "Anybody moves and he's history," he growled. He watched just long enough to see the mobsters quake for a minute, but no one budged.

Then, still holding the MAC-10, he backed silently into the woods.

He'd only gone about thirty paces when a hand touched his shoulder. Frank rounded on the person, his gun raised. Nancy!

At his astounded expression she put a finger to her lips. Then she gestured in the direction of the crash site. They hurried off, making a wide circle around the place where Frank had left the mobsters. "What are you doing here?" he demanded in a low voice.

"I saw you go, and Joe said you were heading for the crash site," she whispered. "I thought you might want company. I tried to catch up with you, but you were moving too fast. It's just as well. If I had caught you, we'd both be in a jam now."

"So *you* were the one who screamed," Frank realized.

She nodded. "I had to distract them. It was the only thing I could think of."

"It worked just fine," Frank said, grinning at her in the darkness. "Thanks!"

Behind them the sound of shouted curses told Frank the gangsters had discovered his absence. "If we're lucky, they may waste some time looking for me in the other direction," he whispered. "But we'll have to hurry."

"So why are we going back to the plane?" Nancy asked him, brushing aside a tree branch that was blocking her path. After he'd explained, she walked on in silence for a few moments before saying, "About the radio, doesn't it seem strange to you that there aren't any rescue teams out looking for our pilot? I mean, you'd think he'd have called for help when he started going down."

Frank hadn't considered that. "Maybe there are rescue teams out, but they just haven't found the plane yet," he suggested.

"I doubt it," Nancy said, shaking her head. "The state police have helicopters. It shouldn't be hard for them to find a downed plane, but no one seems to be looking for it.

"And another thing," she went on. "If Bill was just passing over the mountains on his way to somewhere else, why is he wearing hiking clothes?"

She was right, Frank realized. "Are you saying you think Bill *planned* to crash?"

"I don't know. Maybe. I can't figure out why, but maybe we'll see something at the plane that will tell us more."

At that moment they came to the clearing where the plane was. It lay there like some giant's abandoned toy, glowing white in the moonlight. Luckily the clearing was empty. Apparently the mobsters hadn't found the plane yet.

Running over to it, he climbed in through the hole in the fuselage. When he looked at the control panel, his brown eyes widened in dismay.

The controls were intact, as he had remembered. But where the radio should have been, there was only a gaping hole!

He climbed back out, his thoughts whirling. "There's no radio," he told Nancy, frowning. "If the mobsters got here ahead of us and took it, I can't believe they wouldn't leave someone to guard the plane."

Frank tapped his chin thoughtfully. "I'm beginning to think you're right. Our pal Bill did plan to crash, and he didn't want anyone to know where he was."

"But why?" Nancy asked. "That's what I don't get."

"He could be on the run from the mob," he began, thinking out loud. "Now, what could he have done that would make them send out a small army to get him back?"

"Maybe he stole something from them," Nancy suggested, leaning against the plane. "Something big."

"Good thinking!" Frank said in an excited

whisper. "He stole something of theirs. They tracked him to this area, and now they're hunting him." A frown suddenly creased his forehead. "Only, when Joe and I found him, Bill had nothing on him but the clothes he was wearing. So maybe—"

"Maybe whatever he stole is still in the plane!" Nancy cried, finishing his thought.

"Bingo! I'll check it out." Frank scrambled back into the plane and started looking around, under seats and in storage compartments. He found nothing, not even a scrap of paper.

Suddenly Frank slapped his forehead. "I'm an idiot!" he said. "This is a waste of time."

"Why?" Nancy called from outside.

He jumped out to rejoin her. "The plane's engine burst into flames ten minutes after it went down—Joe and I heard it. When we found Bill, he was lying several feet away from the wreck."

"You're saying he landed the plane, set up a timed charge, and then got out to hide whatever it was he'd stolen," Nancy said. "But why would he be out cold?"

"Maybe he didn't know much about explosives and set the charge too close to himself," Frank answered. He led her to the spot where he and Joe had found the pilot, only about a dozen feet from the plane. "We found him here, lying on his back," he explained. "Maybe he had hidden the loot some-where nearby."

Nancy was already racing toward the edge of the clearing. She flicked her flashlight on and shone it all around. "There's a pile of rocks here that doesn't look natural," she said after a moment.

In an instant Frank was at her side next to a jumbled pile of stones. Both of them began tossing stones aside. Suddenly Nancy let out an excited cry. Reaching into the gap they'd made, she pulled out a large, battered metal suitcase.

It was locked, but Frank knew Nancy was as experienced as he was at getting through locks. In no time she was snapping the catch that held the case closed and flipping up the lid.

"Oh, wow," Frank said softly. "Oh, wow."

The case was packed full of neat bundles of hundred-dollar bills!

Chapter

Fifteen

Nancy nearly dropped the lid of the case, she was so astonished. "Frank, there must be a million dollars in here!"

"At least," he agreed, sounding dazed.

Just then, a faint beam of light swept the air over their heads. Nancy's heart skipped a beat. "The mobsters!" she whispered. "They're coming this way. We've got to get out of here!"

Frank snapped the lid of the suitcase closed. "We can't take this with us. It's too big a risk," he said. "But we should rebury it somewhere else, in case our pilot pal comes for it before we can get it off the mountain.

Nancy nodded and followed him a short distance into the woods. There they made some space in a tangle of old, rotting logs and twigs, put the case in, and carefully covered it.

Frank set an oddly shaped stone next to the spot to mark it.

"If we're lucky, no one will notice the signs of digging," he whispered as they stood up and wiped off their hands.

Nancy held up crossed fingers. "Here's hoping. Now let's get out of here!"

Nancy and Frank headed east up the mountain to rejoin their group. They moved as silently as possible, never speaking even though they didn't hear anyone else nearby. After an hour Nancy guessed they must be far enough away from the mobsters to risk speaking.

"I've been thinking," Nancy whispered to Frank. "For Bill to have been able to pull off a heist like that, he must have had ties to the mob himself. It's got to be an inside job."

"That's about how I see it, too," Frank agreed. His face was in shadow, but Nancy could hear the worry in his voice. "We should definitely hustle back to the group. None of them has any idea how dangerous that guy might be."

Nancy and Frank picked up their pace. Still, the trip up took longer than the trip down. The moon kept dodging behind clouds, leaving them with little or no light to see by. Nancy had brought her flashlight, but they used it only when they absolutely had to. Neither of them wanted to run into another mobster patrol.

Once they passed fairly close to a group of about six men carrying flashlights, and another time they nearly ran into a few more. They must all be part of the group Joe had spotted earlier, Nancy guessed. Luckily they seemed to be heading west, opposite from the group.

Just before Nancy and Frank caught up with the Wilderness trekkers near the summit of the low mountain, where they'd apparently stopped to rest, they hid the MAC-10 in the nearby woods. The trees had thinned out some above them and the open terrain at the exact summit was dominated by giant rock formations.

"Nancy!" George came running up, followed closely by Johnny. "I was so worried! Johnny and I were just getting ready to go search for you."

"We're fine," Nancy assured her, smiling at the way George had said "Johnny and I."

Coach Pemberton strode up, Bill the pilot with him. "There you are!" the coach snapped. "Thanks to you two, we've lost an hour in which we could have been heading down the east slope. Where on earth did you disappear to?"

Frank gave Nancy a subtle wink before he said, "We went back to the plane crash. We wanted to see if the plane radio was working."

As Frank spoke, Nancy carefully watched the pilot. She didn't miss the spark of anxiety that briefly lit his eyes.

"Well, was it?" Coach asked impatiently.

Before Frank could answer, Joe, Curt, and the Shimoya brothers dashed up. "Coach!" Curt cried. "We've been scouting around the summit—"

"And there's a whole line of lights moving up the east side of the mountain," Pete broke in. "They're moving up both sides now!"

Nancy gasped. They were surrounded! The mobsters were working their way up the mountain. It was only a matter of time before the net tightened and they were caught.

"Show me," Coach Pemberton demanded.

The whole group followed as the four boys led the way to a massive cluster of granite domes that formed the summit of the mountain. Each of the domes was far too big to be called a boulder. It was as if the mountain's rocky bones had sprouted up and burst through its skin. The whole formation took up about a quarter mile, shearing off to a cliff on the north end. A small, fast-moving river tumbled down the east slope.

Scrambling to the top of the highest boulder, Joe silently pointed down to the dark slope below. Nancy was near the back of the group. She had to stand on tiptoe to see what he was pointing out. When she saw, her heart sank.

A thin line of glimmering yellow lights spread out horizontally along the slope. From this distance each individual light was so faint that it was hard to tell it was even there. But

Nancy knew that the line was moving up the slope. In a day at the most they'd reach the peak. And there was still the group on the west slope, too. It was just a matter of time before they converged.

"Oh, no," George murmured. She, Johnny, and Melissa were standing in front of Nancy.

The pilot was shaking his head and whistling under his breath. "Those guys know we're up here, and they mean business," he said softly. "I wouldn't want to set the odds on our survival."

Nancy stared at him. Something about what he'd just said made alarm bells ring in her head.

"It sounds like Bill's stopped pretending the mobsters are just a bunch of poachers," came Frank's voice, speaking softly in her ear.

"Yeah," she agreed absently, barely listening. An idea was trying to force its way up from her subconscious. She squeezed her eyes shut and tried to concentrate, but nothing came. Finally, with a sigh of frustration, she gave up.

Coach Pemberton cleared his throat. "It looks like we're surrounded," he said. "Whoever these people are, I'd rather meet them during the day than at night. I think we'd better camp here. No fires, no tents. We'll sleep under the stars. The wind won't be so bad on the other side of those rocks."

"We should post watches, too," Joe said.

"There ought to be at least two people on the lookout for trouble at all times."

Coach seemed about to object, but after glancing down at the lights again, he nodded heavily and said, "Yes, that would be wise."

Pete and Dan volunteered for the first watch. The rest of the group went back to the foot of the rocks, where they'd left their packs, and spread out their sleeping bags.

Checking her watch, Nancy saw that it was now after one in the morning. She rubbed her arms to ward off the heavy chill that had set in. Then, after removing her hiking boots, she slipped gratefully into Pete Shimoya's sleeping bag. Since hers was now at the bottom of that crevasse, the teens had agreed to rotate the bags when they went on watch.

Nancy was so exhausted that she fell asleep almost instantly. It seemed as if only seconds had passed when she was pulled from a deep slumber.

"Wake up, Sleeping Beauty," Frank was saying, shaking her shoulder.

"Mmmph," she mumbled. Then, remembering, she shook herself fully awake. "Oh, the six o'clock watch. Thanks, Frank."

"No problem. Joe's still up there, waiting for you guys to take over," Frank said, making a beeline for his sleeping bag.

Sitting up, Nancy saw George on the sleeping bag next to hers, tying the laces of her hiking boots. Nancy quickly joined her, and the two girls walked the short distance to the rocks at the mountain's peak, where Joe was sitting.

The sky was lightening to a rosy dawn in the east. "Hi, Joe," Nancy greeted him as she and George sat down. "The others will probably be getting up soon, but you might be able to catch some sleep."

"I don't think Coach slept at all," George commented. "I woke up a couple times, and whenever I looked around he was pacing. He even woke up that pilot and talked to him for a while. I bet he wishes he'd agreed to turn back yesterday, when we lost all the food."

Then, like a bolt of lightning, the thought Nancy had been chasing the night before was there. Suddenly everything clicked into place. "That's it!" she cried aloud.

Joe and George both stared at her. "Nan, *what's* it?" George asked. "Are you all right?"

"Joe, go get Frank. We have to talk," Nancy said excitedly. "I just figured something out!"

In less than two minutes he and Frank appeared again. "This better be good, Drew," Frank teased, rubbing his eyes. "I was just dreaming about a hot shower and a steak dinner."

Waving for the Hardys to sit, Nancy turned first to George and Joe. "There are a few things Frank and I found out that you two need to know." She filled them in on finding the suitcase full of money and their suspicion that the pilot had engineered his own plane crash in order to escape from the mob.

When she finished talking, Joe let out a low whistle. "So our Bill's not an innocent victim of the mob. I can't say I'm totally surprised."

"No, but I just figured out something else. . . ." Nancy leaned forward, lowering her voice. "I think Coach Pemberton and the pilot are in this together."

"What!" George, Frank, and Joe all exclaimed.

"How do you figure that?" Frank asked.

"Think about it. Coach is definitely a gambler—the notebook I found proves that. And it was full of bookies' names."

"So?" Joe asked, puzzled.

Nancy continued: "So—who do bookies always work for? Who pulls the strings?"

"The mob. Of course," Frank said slowly. "Bill's a mob bookie."

"Bingo!" Speaking in a rush, Nancy added, "It started to come clear last night, after Bill said something about not wanting to set odds on our making it out of here. That was bookie talk. And then something George said just now, about us not turning back, made it all click.

"All these questions were nagging at me. Why was Coach so firm about our not turning back, even when things were going so badly for us? Why was he so upset when our rescue expedition came back from the crash without any survivors? Why did he try to make everyone think he had a two-way radio, when in fact the one he had was only a receiver?"

"Huh?" Joe asked, confused.

Nancy knew a lot of it didn't make sense to him, since it happened before he and Frank joined the group, but there wasn't time to go over it all now. "Never mind. The details aren't important," she told him. "The main thing is, all these whys suddenly started falling into place."

"There's another why," Frank put in. "Why did Coach Pemberton and Bill seem to know each other? The answer is, they *did* know each other!"

"They *planned* the whole thing. Coach would help Bill get away from the mob, and Bill would give Coach a cut of the money he stole," Nancy said.

"Wow," George added, awestruck. "I don't believe this."

Suddenly a familiar, deep voice cut in behind them. "I wish you hadn't figured it out."

Nancy whirled around. Two shapes loomed above them, black against the rising sun: Coach Pemberton and the pilot. They were each holding a revolver.

"Well, Pemberton," the pilot said, "what's the best way to get rid of four nosy kids on an expedition like this?"

The coach's eyes darted nervously around,

not daring to meet those of Nancy or the others. "I don't know," he muttered at last.

"Know what?" came a new voice.

Nancy jumped as Johnny Alvarez stepped out of the shadows of the rocks, followed by Curt, Melissa, Stasia, Dan, and Pete.

"What's going on?" Johnny broke off as his gaze landed on the revolvers Coach Pemberton and the pilot were holding.

Coach seemed about to speak, but the pilot cut him off. "Shut up!" he snarled.

"What's going on?" Johnny repeated shakily.

"I'll tell you what's going on," Bill snapped. "You shouldn't have poked your noses in here, kids, because now we're going to have to get rid of you all. You just signed your own death warrants!"

Chapter

Sixteen

JOE CLENCHED and unclenched his fists, but he didn't dare make a move—not with two revolvers staring him in the face and a lot of other people around who could get hurt.

"What do you mean?" Johnny asked. His face absolutely white.

Ignoring the question, the pilot merely said, "What should we do with 'em? Toss the whole bunch over the cliff? Shoot them all? Nah, that many bodies, with or without bullets, is bound to raise some questions."

"Looks like you've got a problem there," Joe called. The guy was so arrogant, he couldn't resist making a crack. "Murder's hard to hide."

"Ah, shut up," the pilot growled, waving his gun.

Now Johnny was facing the coach, but Pemberton wouldn't even look at him. Some role model, Joe thought.

"Coach, what's this all about?" Johnny pressed.

"I'll tell you," Nancy spoke up. "This man is on the run from the mob." She pointed at the pilot. "He's a bookie. He told Frank and Joe that his name is Bill, but his real name is Bob Osmian."

Joe nodded. He wasn't sure where Nancy had come up with that name—maybe from the list of bookies she'd mentioned. From the pilot's start of surprise, Joe could tell she was right.

"Excellent. Bob Osmian, at your service," the pilot said with a mocking grin. "You're quite the little detective. Too bad. If you and these two boys"—he waved his gun at Joe and Frank—"had kept out of matters that weren't your business, none of you would be in this fix."

"What?" It was Melissa who had cried out. She shot accusing glares at Joe, Frank, and Nancy.

"Hey, we're not the ones who brought in a hundred mobsters with machine guns," Frank retorted coolly. "This is your mess, Osmian. Don't try to shift the blame to us."

"You mean those mobsters are really after *him?*" Dan Shimoya asked. "Why?"

"Yes, do tell us," Osmian put in, an icy look

in his pale blue eyes. "A few minutes more won't affect my plans. And I must say I'm finding this very interesting."

Glancing at his brother, Joe caught the subtle nod Frank gave him. If they could buy enough time, they might come up with some way out of this mess. Frank was kicking himself for hiding the MAC-10.

"Osmian is a bookie," Frank explained. "He sets odds on horse races, football games, things like that."

"It's all very illegal," Joe put in.

Frank nodded. "That's right. People make bets with him. If they win, he pays them, and if he wins, they pay him. Like most bookies, he's backed by organized crime because there's a lot of money to be made in illegal betting."

"What does any of this have to do with Coach?" Curt broke in.

Joe couldn't help feeling sorry for Curt and Johnny. They were about to learn that their coach was a total creep.

"Coach Pemberton is a gambler," Nancy said, dropping the bombshell. "I suspect he can't help himself—he's compulsive. He bets on everything, including his own team. And to place bets, he needs a bookie. That's how he knows Osmian."

Turning to the coach, Nancy added, "That's what you were using your radio for, too, to keep track of your bets. You didn't want us to know you couldn't use the radio to transmit, so you smashed it yourself."

Coach Pemberton glared at Nancy. "So what if I did?"

"You bet on *us?*" Johnny asked the coach bitterly. "Is that what the team meant to you—extra income? And the players—did you rate us according to how much we were worth? Is that why you made me come on this trip? Because you were losing money on me?"

Their fearless leader said nothing, but a muscle in his jaw fluttered in and out.

"Don't flatter yourself, kid," Osmian said. "High school games are small potatoes. You aren't worth more than a couple of thousand, tops."

Johnny staggered as if he'd been hit, and Curt reached out to steady him. For the first time Joe noticed George's reaction. She was gazing at Johnny as if her heart were breaking for him. Hmm, is there something going on between those two? Joe wondered.

"Anyway," Nancy resumed, "Osmian somehow stole a good deal of cash from his mob bosses. He thought that if he could make it look as though he were dead, the mob wouldn't bother to look for him. So he planned to crash his plane in these mountains, where there wouldn't be any witnesses. He arranged for his friend, Coach Pemberton, to pick him up and guide him out safely."

Turning to the coach, she added, "It was either very daring or very stupid of you to think you could get away with this when all of us were along. Didn't you worry that we'd talk? Or were you planning to get rid of us all the time?"

Pemberton seemed to flinch at that. "I never thought things would go this far," he said in a dull voice. "Osmian came to me last week, after the trip was all arranged. He had this plan, and he wanted my help. I owe him a lot of money, more than I can pay right away. He said if I didn't help him, he'd turn my debts over to his bosses."

The coach swallowed hard, a pleading look in his eyes. "Do you know what the mob does to people who don't pay their debts?"

"We're all crying for you," Frank said angrily from beside Joe. "That still didn't give you the right to endanger everyone here."

"I had to go on with the trip," Coach Pemberton went on in a tortured voice. "It would have looked even stranger if I'd canceled at the last minute. Osmian said he could handle any questions you kids asked, so I left it at that."

"Pemberton's got no guts," Osmian told the teenagers amiably. "Doesn't ask any questions, just shuts his eyes and does as he's told. It's a good quality—too bad you didn't learn it from him while you had the chance."

The group's leader slammed his fist against

his thigh. Glaring at Nancy, Pemberton sputtered, "I knew you were going to be trouble. From the minute you showed up, I could just tell. And then when Curt told me you were a detective! If only you'd taken my warning back at the hotel and gone home, none of this would be happening right now!"

Nancy stared at the coach. Some more things were suddenly fitting together in her mind. "It was you who set that fire in our room," she said. "You tried to burn our gear so we couldn't go."

Coach Pemberton gave Nancy a smug look. "I waited until I saw you leave for the steakhouse, then got the maid to let me in your room. All I had to do was cut the cord and put your packs next to the refrigerator. I figured the fire would do the rest." He frowned. "If the thing had lit up earlier, my plan would have worked."

"So Johnny really was just admiring my pack when he came into our room to borrow soap," George put in.

Johnny didn't seem to hear her or anyone. He was staring at Coach Pemberton, a horrified expression on his face as he burst out, "You set the fire in Nancy and George's room? Does that mean you were the one who set fire to my sleeping bag? And cut my rope and rigged my carabiner so I'd fall? Coach, were *you* the one trying to kill me?"

"What?" Coach looked baffled, then annoyed. "No, no," he said impatiently. "You've been listening to that Drew girl. She fed me the same load of nonsense, about how someone was after you. It's all in her imagination."

Nancy rolled her eyes. It *wasn't* her imagination, but she had to admit she didn't know of any reason why the coach would be out to get Johnny. If Pemberton had actually rigged the path to make it easier for him, why would he then turn around and try to kill Johnny?

Just then Nancy was distracted by Joe, who suddenly straightened up. Tossing his head back, he sniffed the air. Nancy watched curiously as he sniffed again, frowning.

"Hey," he said slowly, "doesn't anyone else smell smoke?"

Nancy did think she caught a faint whiff of wood smoke, mixed with the scent of evergreen trees.

"We didn't light any fires," Stasia said, puzzled.

Just then George gave a cry and pointed down the east slope. "Look! It's a forest fire!"

Nancy's head whipped around, and she stared down the slope. A long line of flames stretched across the mountainside. As she watched, a streak of orange licked up into the sky, then disappeared into the surrounding dark green.

"Those guys think big. They're trying to smoke us out now!" Joe said.

Bob Osmian frowned uncertainly. Then his

face cleared, and he let out a whoop of laughter. "Oh, this is too perfect!" he exclaimed. "There's our answer. Pemberton, get some ropes. We've got to tie these kids up."

Wordlessly the coach handed Osmian his revolver and left the rocks. He reappeared moments later, carrying several coils of the nylon rope the group had been using for rock climbing.

"Boy, Coach really *doesn't* ask any questions, does he?" Joe muttered. "Say, Osmian, what are you planning to do with us?"

"Well, I'll tell you," the bookie answered. He gestured down the east slope with his gun. "This fire could be useful. Fires have a way of destroying evidence that could be embarrassing."

"No fire is hot enough to destroy the evidence a bullet leaves!" George cried.

"We're not going to use bullets," Osmian told her. "We'll just tie you up, take you down the slope, and let the fire do the job. The ropes will burn, and all anyone'll find is a bunch of unfortunate kids who got caught in a forest fire."

Nancy couldn't believe how cruel Osmian was. He sounded as if he were making a shopping list, not planning a multiple murder. "Are you really willing to have ten murders on your conscience?" she asked him. Then, turning to Coach Pemberton, she asked, "Are you?"

The coach stood with his eyes lowered. Then, abruptly, he dropped the rope and turned to Osmian. "I can't do this!" he cried. "There has to be another way."

"Are you nuts?" Osmian snorted without taking his eyes off the teenagers. "If even one of them gets out of here alive, we're sunk."

"By the time the cops are onto us, we'll be long gone. It's a minor risk," the coach pressed. "I can't kill kids in cold blood."

Osmian let out a hollow laugh, saying, "Pemberton, I always thought you were yellow. Lucky for me you gave me your gun." He waved the gun in his left hand at Johnny. "You! Take some of that rope and tie up your pal the coach. I guess he'll just have to burn with you."

Johnny hesitated a moment. Then he picked up a rope and moved toward Coach Pemberton. "Osmian!" Pemberton gasped. "You wouldn't do this to me!"

"Oh, yes, I would, pal." The bookie turned to sneer at Pemberton. "Yes, I would."

Frank saw his opportunity when the bookie's gaze swept away from them. Frank didn't even have to glance at Joe to know he'd seen their chance, too.

Moving at the same instant, he and Joe launched themselves at Osmian. As Frank dived for the guy's right hand, Joe made a grab for Osmian's left. Both of the bookie's arms jerked up in the air as they slammed into him.

One gun flew out of his hand and bounced off into the woods. The other one skittered across the rocks.

After Frank and Joe subdued Osmian, Frank sat on his chest. "I think your plans have been changed," he told Osmian.

"Hold it!" the coach's voice rang out.

Breathing in gulps to catch his breath, Frank looked up—and gasped.

Coach Pemberton had grabbed the second gun when Osmian dropped it. Now he had it aimed at Johnny, who stood frozen in front of him, the rope still dangling from his hands.

Beside Frank, Joe made a hissing noise. Frank knew he was tensed to spring, but there was no way they'd make it to the coach before he could get off a shot.

Frank's attention was riveted on Johnny, whose fear Frank could almost feel. I hope this guy has guts when it counts, thought Frank. Because Johnny's the only one who can stop Pemberton now!

Chapter

Seventeen

JOE HELD HIS BREATH as Johnny, moving slowly, placed the coiled rope on the ground. "You won't shoot me, Coach," Johnny said quietly. "You couldn't."

Drops of perspiration were running off Pemberton's forehead into his eyes. "I wouldn't advise putting that to the test," he said. "Back off, Alvarez."

To Joe's amazement, Johnny held firm. "Give me the gun, Coach," Johnny said in a steady voice. He took a step forward, holding out his hand.

"I said, back off!" Pemberton shouted.

Johnny took another step. "Give me the gun," he repeated.

Joe tensed as Coach Pemberton's finger tightened on the trigger. Joe wanted to yell for

160

Johnny to stop, but he was afraid he might startle the coach into firing.

Then the coach wavered. Johnny was only an arm's length from him now. Reaching out, he simply removed the gun from the coach's unresisting fingers.

"Coward!" Osmian snapped.

Johnny turned around, holding the gun loosely. His face was glowing with pride and confidence. "All right!" Joe cheered.

All the teenagers burst into a spontaneous round of applause, and tears of relief streamed down some of their faces. Joe couldn't help noticing that George clapped and whooped the loudest and longest.

Nancy, Frank, and Joe made short work of tying up Osmian and Pemberton. As Nancy cut lengths to tie Coach's hands, she kept sniffing at the rope.

"Does it smell funny?" Joe asked her.

"No, that's the weird thing," Nancy answered, frowning. "It just smells like rope. Before, my rope smelled different."

Joe gave her a curious look before returning his attention to binding Osmian's hands and feet. Whatever Nancy was talking about could wait until they had figured out how to get down off this mountain alive.

After they'd finished tying up the prisoners, the group held a quick meeting to plan their next move. There were the spreading fire and mobsters to deal with. Sooner or later someone would report the fire, but they couldn't afford to wait for help.

"We've got a little time yet. Let's split up into teams," Frank suggested. "We'll leave a few people on guard. The rest of us will scout the north, west, and south slopes to see what our options are." He nodded down the eastern slope, where the fire was advancing the most quickly. "Heading east is obviously out of the question."

Johnny, Melissa, and Stasia stayed behind to guard the prisoners. Frank and Pete went north, while Nancy, Dan, and Curt headed west. Joe found himself paired with George and heading down the north slope.

"Go quietly," he said to her. "We don't want to run into any—" He broke off as he heard a faint shuffling in the woods ahead of them. Someone was disturbing the pine needles blanketing the ground.

"Shhh! What's that?" Joe pulled George behind a big tree, and they stood still, barely breathing.

Two minutes later a tall, thin man came tromping by, dragging a rifle behind him. "Who needs it?" he was muttering. "Traipsing around on a stupid mountain, hunting a small-time bookie. I got better things to do!"

I guess the bosses haven't told anyone about the million-plus dollars that the "small-time" bookie stole, Joe reflected.

Suddenly George touched his arm. Her

brown eyes danced with excitement as she pointed to the walkie-talkie that protruded from the pocket of the gangster's jacket.

She wants to steal the mobster's walkie-talkie! Joe realized. He might have hesitated to suggest it, but since George was game . . .

He nodded. Just as the mobster made it past them, Joe shot forward in one sweeping motion and seized the guy's rifle. Continuing the movement, he brought it up and around, clubbing the guy with the butt. The guy fell without a sound—he was out cold.

George retrieved the walkie-talkie. "Nice work, partner," she told him.

"Thanks to you," Joe replied, grinning.

Just then the sound of men's voices drifted to them. "It must be the rest of our guy's patrol," Joe whispered. "Quick, we'd better hide him. Otherwise, they'll know we're around."

He and George swiftly dragged the unconscious man into a slight hollow behind a boulder. They left him there, minus his rifle. The gun would be extra insurance. Then they hurried away.

"This whole mountain is crawling with men," George said nervously. "We'll never get through their net, not with twelve people, two of whom are tied up."

"We'll make it," Joe said reassuringly. "We have a really good chance, now that we've got this walkie-talkie. Come on, let's head back to camp. With any luck we can switch the frequency and use it as a radio."

When they got back to camp, half an hour after they'd left, the other patrols had already reported in. From the discouraged looks on everyone's faces, Joe guessed the news wasn't good.

"We have less time than we thought," Nancy reported. "Whatever we do, we'd better do it fast."

Joe held out the walkie-talkie. "George and I, ah, borrowed this from a 'friend,'" he said. "Frank, do you know how to switch the frequency so these goons won't hear our transmission?"

Frank's eyes lit up. "Can do," he said, taking it from Joe.

"Hey, nice going!" Johnny complimented Joe and George, pounding them both on the back. George coughed and blushed.

"You're the real hero," a female voice purred in Joe's ear. Startled, he turned and found himself staring into Melissa's dark, pretty eyes. "Getting that walkie-talkie might save our lives."

Was it his imagination, or was Melissa turning the charm on, full force. Joe grinned back, and a second later he felt himself being pulled aside.

"Don't fall for it, Joe," Nancy whispered in his ear. "Melissa's just playing games to get Johnny mad."

"Oh—uh, right." Joe glanced back at Melissa, who was glaring openly at Johnny and George. Johnny didn't seem to notice. Flashing a quick smile at Nancy, Joe said, "You mean it wasn't my irresistible charm?"

"Got it!" Frank announced suddenly. Joe and Nancy both turned to him. "I hope, that is." Frank held up the walkie-talkie to Joe. "Want to give it a try?"

Joe took it and twisted the dial, searching for a working frequency. Strange crackles and whistles came out of the thing. Then, suddenly, Joe heard voices—and in the background a *beat-beat-beat* that could only be the whirring of a helicopter's rotors.

Yes! he thought triumphantly. "Hello!" he cried into the mike. "Hello! Can anyone read me?"

"Hello!" came an answering voice. "Who's that? You're on the wrong frequency, pal. Ground patrols shouldn't be on this one."

"Joe!" Frank whispered. "Be careful. That sounds like one of the mobsters."

Joe nodded. His heart was thudding in his chest. If he made one false move, their entire group was in big trouble.

"Hey—who's there?" the voice demanded again.

"Uh—this is Callahan," Joe said, trying to imitate the peculiar, soft voice of the gangster he and Frank had encountered two days earlier.

"Callahan?" the voice on the radio repeated. "What happened to your voice? You sound funny."

"Uh—a cold. It's from being out all night in the woods," Joe said quickly.

"Yeah, yeah," the voice crackled back. "So what do you want?"

Joe shot a rapid glance at Frank and Nancy. What he was about to do was awfully risky, and he hadn't discussed it with them. But he couldn't think of any other way to get out of the mess they were in.

"Hey, listen, I got Osmian," he said. Out of the corner of his eye, he saw the bookie's eyes widen in fear. "He can't walk, though—his leg's broken. We're up on the peak, in a cluster of rocks. I need someone to airlift us out of here."

"You got him, eh?" The voice sounded disappointed. "How's about splitting the bounty money with me?"

Joe grinned. The mobster had bought his story! "If you get us out of here, I'll split it fifty-fifty with you," Joe promised.

"All right, I'm on my way. Over and out," the copter pilot said.

Joe flicked off the walkie-talkie and turned to the others, giving them the thumbs-up sign. "How's that for service?" he crowed as several of the group whistled and clapped approvingly.

"You were terrific, Joe," Nancy said, patting

him on the shoulder. "But how are you going to explain the rest of us when he gets here?"

"I figure we'll cross that bridge when we get to it," Joe told her. "I didn't want to mention extra people, in case he got suspicious."

Joe turned toward his brother as Frank spoke up. "I have a plan. Joe and I'll wait for the copter. Joe can pretend to be Callahan, and I'll say I'm Osmian. Once we get the guy on the ground, we should be able to 'persuade' him to help us." Frank held up the MAC-10, which he'd recovered. "The rest of you take cover and keep out of sight."

Johnny slapped Curt and Dan on the back. "We'll be back up if you need it."

Whatever had been tearing the group apart before was gone now. They were working well together, Joe realized. Judging by the smile Nancy gave the guys, she was happy, too.

As the group was scattering, Joe could hear the faint *beat-beat* of the chopper's rotors. He and Frank moved over to a tall tree. In its shadow their features would be hard to make out.

"You'd better lie down," he told Frank. "You're supposed to have a broken leg, remember?"

Frank obediently lay down on the rocks, his body over the automatic. The copter's rotors grew steadily louder. "Hey, Joe," Frank said after a minute.

"Yeah?"

Frank reached up and gripped his brother's hand. "Be careful."

Joe nodded, suddenly tense. There was no time to answer—the copter was rising above the edge of the rock in front of them, only about fifty feet away. It hovered there for a moment, like some monstrous insect. Then it began its descent.

A squawk sounded from Joe's walkie-talkie. Switching on the mike, he said, "Callahan here."

"Hey, where are you?" the copter pilot complained. "I don't see you."

"I'm under a tree to your left," Joe told the pilot. "It was hot in the sun."

"Where?" the pilot demanded. "I still don't see you. The sun's in my eyes. Wave, would you?"

Reluctantly, Joe waved his arm. He could see the outline of a single person in the helicopter's cockpit.

"Oh, okay, I got you," the pilot's voice came back over the speaker. "Listen, I can't land on these rocks. I'm going to move in closer, hover low, and let the ladder down. You'll have to carry Osmian out to it."

Joe and Frank exchanged worried glances. "He can't land?" Joe echoed. "What do we do now?"

Frank shrugged. "Improvise, little brother."

The copter moved closer, until the wind from the rotors was tossing Joe's hair and blowing dust into his eyes. He raised his hands, squinting.

Suddenly the walkie-talkie squawked again, as the pilot cried, "Hey, you're not Callahan!"

They were found out!

"Run for it, Joe!" Frank yelled, jumping to his feet.

Joe was already dashing for the helicopter. He reached it a step ahead of Frank and flung himself onto one of the landing skids. Frank grabbed the other one just as the copter was lifting off. "Whoa!" Joe cried, grasping for a hold.

The helicopter rose quickly. Then the pilot began turning the craft violently from side to side. Joe locked his fingers around a steel support strut, but each sudden movement threw him dangerously out to the side.

"Brace yourself, Frank!" he shouted over the deafening whir of the chopper's blades. "It's going to be a wild ride!"

Chapter

Eighteen

FRANK GRITTED HIS TEETH and clung to the copter's runner with all his strength. Most of his body hung below the skid, and he thrashed wildly from side to side as the craft swooped and dipped.

If he didn't get aboard in the next thirty seconds, he was going to fall!

His body steadied a little as the copter stopped swinging and rose smoothly into the air. He's sending the bird aloft for another dive, Frank realized. Now's my chance!

A few moments later the helicopter dived sharply. Frank used the momentum to jackknife his body up above the landing skid. Then he scissored his legs around the skid, so he was sitting on it, with his ankles locked together below it.

Breathing hard, he glanced worriedly over to the other runner, then smiled. Joe was securely seated on it, grinning at him.

The loud roar of the copter made it impossible to talk. Frank gestured with his chin toward the copter doors to signal his plan: Each of them would climb up through the helicopter's side openings and surprise the pilot.

Joe nodded his understanding and let go with one hand to flash Frank the thumbs-up. The pilot had stopped trying to throw Frank and Joe. He probably figured he had succeeded.

The wind whipped Frank's hair and brought tears to his eyes as he pulled his feet up to crouch on the helicopter's landing skid. Gripping the metal supports that connected the skids to the helicopter's body, he hazarded a glance down and gulped at the sight of trees and rocks far below. A river that started near the peak wound down the east side of the mountain, he saw in a flash, and the fire was definitely advancing. He and Joe had to work fast!

Frank's hands felt the metal lip at the outer edge of the door, and he used it to pull himself up to stand. Finally he could see in through the window in the upper half of the helicopter door. Joe's head was already visible through the window on the other side, his eyes gleaming with anticipation.

The pilot was on Joe's side, the top of his

seat back just a few inches in front of Joe. Blond hair stuck out from beneath the baseball cap the pilot wore. If he turned his head even slightly, he'd be staring right into Joe's eyes, but the pilot didn't seem to have noticed a thing. He stared straight ahead, a pistol on the passenger seat next to him.

Frank reached for the door handle and slowly eased it down until he felt it click open, thankful that the whirring of the rotors drowned out the noise. Then he maneuvered his body to the side so that he'd be able to jump in when he swung the door open. He kept his gaze fastened on the pilot the whole time. Frank gave Joe a quick nod.

Instantly Joe flung open the door on his side and heaved himself up and inside the helicopter, just behind the pilot.

The pilot whipped around, shock on his face. "What—!" he yelled, pushing Joe backward.

Frank gasped as his brother was nearly thrown back out the side of the helicopter, barely managing to grab hold of the sides of the doorway.

Frank didn't waste a second. He pulled open his door and was just swinging himself up and inside when the pilot reached for the gun on the passenger seat. Frank snatched it up before the pilot could get to it and pressed the muzzle against the guy's neck.

After that it was an easy matter to persuade

the pilot to bring the helicopter down. They landed on a flat area behind the dome rocks. Frank handed the gun to Joe and jumped out to get the others.

"Great going!" Nancy said, running to meet them. But Frank noticed an uneasy look in her blue eyes. "Uh, I don't think all of us are going to fit in that thing," she added.

That thought had already occurred to him. "I know," Frank told her. "Don't worry, I have it all worked out." He hoped he sounded more confident than he felt. He did have a plan, but it was risky.

She waved back toward the surrounding trees, and the rest of their group came out of hiding, lugging their packs. Johnny and Curt led Osmian and Coach Pemberton, whose hands were still bound. Stooping, they ran to the helicopter.

Stasia, Melissa, Pete, and Dan were already inside when the pilot protested, "Are you nuts? I can't fly this thing with all these people!"

"How many can it take?" Frank asked. Joe prodded the pilot with the gun. "Be honest, now."

The pilot flinched. "Seven, maybe eight at the most," he answered. "Including me."

Frank nodded. "We'll take only one back-pack," he said, turning to the others. "You can all stow your wallets and anything that's really important in it. Five of us will have to stay

173

behind," he continued, as everyone moved to follow his instructions. "To start with, I volunteer our two prisoners."

"Hey!" Osmian cried. "You can't do that to me! I demand to be put on that helicopter!"

"You don't have a choice," Frank told him. With a grin he added, "But if it makes you feel better, I'm staying, too."

"Me, too," Nancy put in promptly.

"And me!" Joe chimed in. He handed the gun to Curt and climbed down from the helicopter.

"What about me?" Johnny asked in an indignant voice. "I'm not going to leave you guys in the lurch after all you've done for us."

"Me, either," George added. "If you think I'm going to go off without you, Nancy Drew, you've got another thing coming!"

Nancy shook her head. "Someone has got to get to the police, and you two are elected," she told George and Johnny. "Besides, we'll be fine. Frank's got a foolproof plan for saving our necks. Don't you, Frank?"

If only it *was* foolproof! Taking a deep breath, Frank replied, "Sure thing. Coach Pemberton, have you ever done any whitewater rafting?"

The coach had been staring morosely down at the rocks the whole time. Now he raised his eyes with a start. "Huh? I've done some. Why?"

Frank led Joe, Nancy, George, Johnny, and

their two prisoners to the edge of the rocks, where the river roared out and spilled down the mountain's east side. "When I was up in the air, I saw that little river. It runs all the way down the mountain," he said.

"What?" George gasped. "You mean you're going to brave those?" She pointed at some rocks in the far bank. Water churned furiously around them.

Frank shrugged. "I don't think we have any choice."

"Hold on!" Coach Pemberton said, alarmed. "You may think it looks bad up here, but let me tell you, this is nothing compared to what the water's like half a mile downstream. Trying to raft down this river is asking for trouble."

"More trouble than we're already in?" Joe asked pointedly. Scowling, the coach snapped his mouth shut.

Frank turned and strode back to the helicopter. "You guys," he called in. "We're going to need your help to put together a raft."

Everyone but Curt, who was guarding the helicopter pilot, pitched in. Soon they had lashed together a crude framework of branches, over which two yellow tent canvases were stretched. Frank, Joe, and Nancy each took an aluminum tent pole to push the raft away from any rocks.

"I think you're taking an awful chance," George commented when the raft was done.

Nancy definitely felt uneasy but just said, "We'll be fine. Come on, you guys better go."

Reluctantly George and Johnny climbed aboard the helicopter. A moment later the engine whirred on, and the loud beat of the copter's blades made talking impossible. The craft lumbered heavily as it took off. For one breathless moment Nancy thought it wasn't going to get airborne, but finally it did and headed off toward the east.

As the noise of the helicopter receded, a heavy silence fell over the rest of them. Looking down the eastern slope, Nancy saw tongues of flame licking up into the sky not more than a half-mile away. The smell of smoke was much stronger now.

At last Joe broke the silence. "Okay, big brother. Let's see how this scheme of yours works out." His voice was light, but Nancy noticed he was staring at the fire, too.

They untied Osmian and Coach. It didn't seem likely that either of them would try any funny business now, when they needed Nancy and the Hardys to help them escape. If the water got rough, they would need to use their hands.

Joe knotted the pieces of rope together, coiled the rope, and tied the coil around his waist like a belt. "You never know when this might come in handy," he said.

"Well, guys, let's do it," Frank said, and Nancy nodded her agreement. They decided to leave the MAC-10 and rifle behind and take only one revolver, which Joe stuck into his belt. The five of them waded into the icy, rushing water, pushing their raft in front of them. Frank held the raft in place while everyone else climbed aboard. Finally he got on, too, and they were off.

There was barely room on the raft for the five of them. Nancy glanced back regretfully at the pile of packs on the bank of the river. They'd brought nothing with them but some trail mix and dried fruit.

"Boy, what I wouldn't give for a hot shower and a cooked meal right now," Joe said.

Nancy couldn't help giggling at the forlorn way he stared at the trail mix in his hand. "Don't tell me you've had enough of this nature stuff, Joe."

"Don't tell me you *haven't* had enough," Joe retorted. Just then a spray of cold water shot over the side of the raft, soaking his trail mix. Nancy and Frank burst out laughing. A smile spread across Joe's face as he said, "All I can say is, I'd better get a bacon cheeseburger by tonight, or I won't be held responsible for my actions!"

"We ought to find some town by then," Nancy said. *If we make it,* she added silently.

The raft shot downriver, flashing past rocks and tree branches on either side. Fortunately, there seemed to be a channel in the middle of the water, so the going was fairly smooth.

As they descended, the smoke got thicker. Soon they were all coughing, and Nancy felt her eyes watering. She could feel the heat of the fire, too, drying her lips and scorching her throat. Flames crackled in the forest around them.

Suddenly Frank let out a cry from the front of the raft. "Rocks ahead!"

Nancy moved to the front of the wobbly craft as quickly as she could. When she saw what Frank was pointing at, she felt a chill, despite the heat of the fire.

Directly ahead of them, the river narrowed. Water foamed and boiled around a string of jagged rocks that stretched across the river like giant's teeth. Beyond those the water was entirely white. Nancy knew that meant more rocks were just under the surface.

The swifter current snatched the raft, and it shot forward with a jerk, causing Nancy to stumble backward. She used the tent pole to steady herself, then dropped to her knees beside Frank, her pole at the ready.

Behind her, Joe whooped, "Here we go!"

"Hold on to your hats!" Frank shouted. As the raft plunged past the first line of rocks, he lunged with his pole to push them past a rock.

Suddenly behind them Osmian let out a furious yell. "Get off me, you ox! What are you trying to do, throw me overboard?"

"I wasn't doing anything to you. Don't

push!" Coach sounded panicky. "Cut that out! Hey—help! He's trying to kill me!"

The raft started to rock violently. Nancy looked over her shoulder. "Oh, no," she groaned. Osmian and Coach Pemberton were locked in combat, each clawing at the other's throat.

"Stop it!" Nancy yelled, as the raft tipped sharply. "You're going to capsize us!"

It was too late. Even as she yelled the warning, Coach threw himself at Osmian's knees. Both men fell over, landing on one corner of the raft. The flimsy craft tipped sideways.

Nancy let out a scream as all five of them were hurled into the churning white water!

Chapter

Nineteen

Nancy's scream was cut short as the foaming water closed over her head.

For a moment she couldn't move, stunned by the ice-cold water. Finally, still submerged, she began thrashing at the water, but her feet couldn't find the bottom. Her lungs felt as if they would burst.

Get a grip, Drew! Opening her eyes, she looked for where the water was lightest, then swam toward that. In a moment her head broke the surface.

She sputtered, gasping for breath. Through the rushing water she saw two other heads bobbing nearby. She started to call out to them, but a powerful surge of water struck her just then, filling her mouth. The current was dragging her downstream.

"Yikes!" Nancy yelled as something big and yellow suddenly loomed in front of her. Then she realized what it was. The raft!

It was tilted at a slight angle and wedged now between two rocks. In a flash Nancy was racing past it. Shooting her hands out, she grabbed the edge. The strong current threatened her grip, but she managed to pull herself around to the downstream side of the raft, where she was sheltered from the full force of the rushing water.

"Joe!" she yelled at the top of her lungs. "Frank! Where are you? Are you all right?"

There was no answer. "Joe! Frank!" Nancy repeated, fighting down fear.

Then, on the far side of the raft, a hand shot up out of the water. It was followed by another hand, and then a head. Frank's. Nancy was so relieved she felt tears spring to her eyes.

"Are you all right?" she asked him.

"I think so," he said, coughing. "Have you seen Joe?"

"Hey!" a faint voice called. "Over here!"

Nancy and Frank both whipped around at the same instant. She spotted a bedraggled, blond-haired figure clinging to a boulder on the far side of the river. The figure waved wearily.

"It's Joe!" Nancy cried. "He's okay!"

Frank said nothing, but Nancy saw a wide smile spread across his face.

Suddenly she remembered their two prisoners. Pushing her soaked hair from her face, she looked urgently around. She didn't see anyone else in the river, and soon the shore would be a mass of flaming trees. Already the smoke was making her eyes water. "Frank, what about Coach and Osmian? I don't see either of them!"

"Neither do I," Frank replied.

"You don't think . . ." Nancy's voice trailed off.

Frank drew his brows together in a frown. "The three of us are okay, aren't we? So maybe they are, too," he said hopefully. "They must have been washed downriver; otherwise we'd see them. If we can get going again, maybe we'll be able to find them."

"I hope so," Nancy murmured, her teeth beginning to chatter from the cold.

"You'd better get out of the water," Frank said, critically studying her from the other side of the raft. "Your lips are almost the same shade of blue as your eyes. Not that your eyes aren't a nice color . . ." he hastened to add.

Nancy couldn't help laughing. "Thanks for the compliment, Frank. Now, just how are we supposed to get out of the water?"

"First of all we need to right the raft," Frank said. "Here—you push on your side, and I'll pull here. Okay?"

Nancy braced her booted feet against one of the boulders that was holding the raft in place.

Then she pushed. With a grating noise the raft moved, then abruptly popped free. It was no longer wedged, but the big rocks still prevented it from being carried downriver.

"Good. Now I'll hold the raft steady," Frank said. "Can you climb up?"

"I think so," Nancy said between clenched teeth. She was so cold it was hard to make her muscles obey her, but she managed to pull herself up onto the yellow canvas. She lay still for a second, gasping.

When she was safely aboard, Frank hauled himself up. The two of them gazed across to where Joe still clung to his boulder.

"He's only thirty feet away, but it might as well be a mile," Frank muttered, his lips tight. "How are we going to get him back?"

"If only we had a rope," Nancy said, thinking aloud. Then she snapped her fingers. "Hey, we do! That is, Joe does—if he didn't lose it in the water. He saved the ones we tied Coach and Osmian up with, remember?"

Frank grabbed Nancy's shoulders excitedly. "You're right. If he still has it, maybe he can throw it to us and we can make a guide rope to help him across to us."

Both of them rose to their knees, waving their arms to get Joe's attention. "Joe!" Frank yelled. "Do you still have that rope?"

"It's all I have—I lost the revolver." Joe pulled the coil from around his waist and flourished it over his head.

"Can you throw an end to us?" Nancy shouted over the loudly rushing water.

"I'm not sure it's long enough," Joe called back. "But I'll give it a shot." He looped one end around the boulder he was perched on and tied it securely. Then he twirled the free end over his head and let it fly.

The rope sailed through the air and splashed into the water upriver from the raft. The powerful current grabbed it and swept it downstream.

"Uhngh!" Frank grunted as he lunged for the end. He missed, but Nancy was able to grab it as it sailed by her.

"Got it!" she cried triumphantly. Her spirits sank a moment later, however, when she saw that the rope wasn't long enough to loop around any of the boulders on their side. "It won't reach."

"It *has* to," Frank said in a determined voice. Taking the rope end from her, he made a small loop in it, which he knotted in place with a bowline. Then he put the loop around his wrist.

"Frank Hardy, what are you doing?" Nancy cried as he lowered himself into the icy water.

He grinned at her. "Making the rope reach." Holding on to the edge of the raft, he inched downstream. He wrapped his free arm and one leg around one of the boulders that held the raft in place. "Okay, Joe!" he yelled across the river. "Can you pull yourself across now?"

Nancy's mouth fell open. Frank was making himself a human anchor for Joe! "Just don't let go of that rock, Frank," she warned him. "If you get washed away, I'll never forgive you!"

Frank managed a slight smile. Then Nancy saw his jaw tighten as the rope went taut. Joe had started across.

Slowly he made his way over. The frothing water dragged at his body, trying to tear him away from the lifeline. As she watched, Nancy hardly breathed. "Come on, Joe," she muttered.

Then, suddenly, he was across, and Nancy was hauling both him and Frank back aboard the raft. The brothers sprawled there, gasping and shivering. Part of Joe's red plaid shirt had been ripped away, and he had a huge rent running down the leg of his jeans.

After a moment he opened his eyes. "Whew," he said. "I wanted a hot shower, not a cold Jacuzzi."

Nancy giggled, and a moment later all three of them were clutching their sides, laughing.

Suddenly the raft gave a lurch. "Whoa," Nancy said, dropping flat onto the canvas. "We're coming unwedged. Hang on, guys!"

They all lay flat as the raft broke free and started spinning down the rapids once again. They'd lost their poles when they capsized, so there was nothing much they could do to control the raft except hang on and hope for the best.

The raft leapt down the turbulent river, bucking and tossing like a wild horse. But after about ten minutes the movements seemed a bit calmer. Cautiously Nancy peered ahead.

"Guys!" she said excitedly. "I think we're at the end of the rapids!" Smooth water stretched in a broad sweep in front of them.

"She's right," Joe commented, turning to grin at Nancy.

"Hey, what's that thing hanging over that branch there?" Frank said suddenly. He pointed at a downed tree just ahead of the raft. Its branches were sticking up out of the water, and something greenish black was draped over them.

"Let's find out," Nancy suggested. As the raft slid by, she grabbed for the thing and pulled it on deck. It was a swath of green plaid cloth, cold and saturated with water. Nancy shivered. She'd seen that cloth before.

"It's Osmian's shirt," she said in a low voice. "Guys, we never did pass him or Coach. I wonder if they made it out of the rapids."

After a long silence Frank said, "There's no way of knowing. As soon as we get out of here, we'll send a search party back for them."

Nancy nodded, staring soberly out over the water. No one spoke as they continued to drift on down the river, but she knew the Hardys must be thinking the same thing she was—that the chances of the coach and Osmian making it past the rapids and the fires and the mobsters weren't very great.

"Look!" Joe said excitedly, gazing at the thick evergreens on either side of the river. "What's different about this picture?"

Frank shot his brother an annoyed glance. "Stop playing games, Joe."

"No smoke, no flames," Joe continued.

Nancy perked up immediately. "We're through the fire!" she exclaimed. "I was so relieved to be alive after those rapids, I didn't even notice. We can go ashore now. We made it!"

"Amazing," was all Frank said. "Let's go."

They beached the raft at the next bend they came to and splashed ashore. "Civilization, here we come," Joe said, stretching out his arms.

Nancy turned for a last look at the river. It was so peaceful here, with no sound except the gurgling water and the gentle rustling of trees.

A twig snapped behind her, and Nancy started to turn around, tensing automatically. The click of a gun's safety catch being withdrawn a moment later made her freeze in her tracks.

"Good morning, kids," said a soft voice. "We meet again."

Nancy turned slowly, her heart in her throat. She found herself facing a circle of guns—six of them—and they were all aimed at her, Frank, and Joe.

Chapter

Twenty

THE SIX MOBSTERS closed in on them as Nancy's heart sank. Even if she and the Hardys somehow managed to disarm these guys, they were still outnumbered two to one.

"You remember me and my pal Lorenzo, don't you, boys?" the man with the soft voice asked. He waved one hand at the tall, beefy man next to him, but his small, dark eyes remained steadily on Frank and Joe. "We've got a score to settle."

"Callahan, isn't it?" Frank said. "You goon."

"I wouldn't exactly say we have a score to settle," Joe chimed in. "Taking down scum like you is just par for the course for us."

Lorenzo let out a growl, but Callahan

slapped the muzzle of his gun against the big man's chest. "Easy. They're just talking tough, that's all."

Nancy was beginning to understand the Hardys' game. Callahan and Lorenzo must be the two guys Frank and Joe had disarmed and tied up right after they'd rescued Osmian from the phony plane crash. Frank and Joe were trying to make them angry enough to get careless. It was an incredible risk, but she could see it was their only chance.

"So these are the bozos you were talking about, huh, Frank?" she asked with a toss of her head. "Even Osmian was making cracks about them."

Lorenzo, furious, threw his gun to the ground and snarled, "I'll tear you apart with my bare hands."

"Cut it out," Callahan ordered sharply. "Remember, no matter how fast these punks are with their fists, they can't outrun a bullet."

Lorenzo mulled that over for a minute. At last an ugly smile spread over his lips. "Right, Mr. Callahan," he said, picking up his gun again.

Nancy stifled a sigh of disappointment. Suddenly a flash of movement over Callahan's shoulder caught her eye. Someone in a striped T-shirt had just darted behind a tree.

"What should we do with them?" Callahan was facing another mobster, a wiry man with close-cropped gray hair. "These kids are a handful, I can tell you that from personal experience. Should we get rid of 'em now?"

"Maybe we should hang on to them," the wiry thug suggested. "If they know where Osmian is, the boss'll want to talk to them."

Trying not to appear obvious, Nancy craned her neck to peer into the shadowy woods. Just then a head of dark short hair peeked out from behind another tree, and a hand waved at Nancy.

George! How had she gotten there? And how many were with her? As if reading Nancy's mind, George held up four fingers. It was all Nancy could do to keep her face immobile. She didn't dare look at the thugs for fear the glow in her eyes would give them all away. Help had arrived!

Nancy had to keep the mobsters distracted so they wouldn't notice George and the others. Mustering all her acting skills, she forced tears to her eyes and made her lower lip tremble. "I can't stand this!" Nancy cried. "Osmian told us all about the money. If I tell you everything, will you let us go?"

"Nancy!" Joe cried. Frank was staring at her as if she had suddenly sprouted an extra head.

Callahan and the gray-haired man exchanged glances. "Why don't you tell us what you know, and then we'll talk terms," Callahan suggested after a moment. Nancy noticed that both he and the gray-haired man had lowered their guns.

Behind him Nancy could see stealthy movement among the trees. George and the others were moving up.

"Okay," Nancy said in a desperate voice. "Here goes. When Osmian crashed he had a metal suitcase full of cash with him."

"Nancy, shut up!" Frank said through clenched teeth. But Nancy knew from the slow wink he gave her that he had spotted George as well.

"Osmian hid the case at the bottom of a deep ravine," she went on. "I could take you there—"

"Only you might fall and hurt yourselves!" Joe cried. He and Frank sprang forward, hurling themselves at Callahan and the gray-haired man. Nancy was right with them, shooting out her leg in a karate kick that knocked the gun from the gangster nearest her.

At the same instant George, Johnny, Curt, and Dan popped up behind the other three mobsters. They reached around them, their hands full of gritty mud from the riverbank, which they rubbed into the thugs' eyes.

Nancy was about to help them when the gangster she had disarmed leapt at her. She lashed out with a second kick that sent him sprawling. As she picked up his gun, Frank's voice said, "I've got your guy covered, Nan."

Nancy turned to see that Frank was holding the gun he'd gotten from Callahan, and he was pointing it at the guy Nancy had knocked down. Joe had another gun trained on Callahan and the gray-haired thug.

The other three mobsters had dropped their guns but were still struggling with George, Johnny, Dan, and Curt. Nancy jumped in to help. Within seconds all six of the thugs were on the ground with their hands behind their backs.

Nancy collected the fallen weapons and dumped all but two of them into the river. Frank and Joe each kept the ones they'd wrested from Callahan and the gray-haired man. That would be sufficient to keep the group under control.

Joe faced Callahan, a cocky grin on his face. "Yes, we met again. And once again, we won—"

"Joe," Nancy cut in. "There's no need to gloat. And besides, you had a lot of help this time!" As George came over to them, Nancy gave her a big hug.

"Yeah, where did you guys come from?" Frank wanted to know. "Aren't you supposed to be in a helicopter on your way to the police?"

"Well, the helicopter really wasn't flying too well with all of us in it," George began.

Johnny cut in, his eyes twinkling. "The real

truth is, we figured if you could shoot the rapids on a raft, we could meet you at the bottom. We made the copter pilot put us down near here—"

"But we left Melissa, Stasia, and Pete to take him to the cops," Curt added. He put one hand to his ear. "In fact, I think I hear them now." He smiled mischievously at the mobsters. "Hear that helicopter, guys? We told our friends to tell the police to send additional helicopters for you and us. They're sending police in on the ground, too."

Nancy saw Callahan flinch.

"Not to mention fire fighters for that blaze you guys set," Dan said.

"After we heard and saw you," George said, beaming, "I asked myself, 'What would Nancy or Frank or Joe do in this situation?' And that's how we came up with our plan to rescue you."

Nancy hugged George again. "Brilliant!" she declared. "That's the second time you've saved my life during this trip."

"She's something, isn't she?" Johnny said, grinning. Bright red spots rose to George's cheeks, and Nancy knew how pleased she was by the compliment.

Just then a helicopter came into view above them. "This is the police!" an amplified voice boomed. "Lay down your weapons."

* * *

"I'll be back in a half hour or so," Frank called. "I'm just going out to look around, maybe buy some postcards."

"Take your time," Joe replied through the bathroom door. "I'm going to take the longest, hottest shower in the history of man."

He heard Frank chuckle, then the door of their hotel room clicked shut. With a sigh of pleasure Joe stepped into the steaming hot shower.

It had been a long, hard day, he reflected. You'd think that after all they'd been through the police would have let them rest up a little, or at least would have given them a decent meal. But all they'd gotten at the state police headquarters was lukewarm tea or coffee and soggy ham sandwiches.

Each of the ten teenagers had had to give a complete statement. Then an FBI man had arrived and grilled Nancy, Frank, and Joe for hours about Osmian and the other mobsters. It seemed the FBI had been after both Osmian and Callahan for some time, as well as the mysterious boss Callahan had referred to.

That FBI agent wasn't very grateful, either, Joe mused as he scrubbed himself. He seemed to take it personally that Osmian had vanished in the rapids. "We wanted that guy," the agent kept saying. "Boy, did we want that guy!"

At least the FBI agent had seemed happy that the police helicopters had managed to round up the other gangsters. By the time Joe and the other kids were allowed to leave, over forty of them had been brought in. The remaining handful would be picked up by the police that had gone up into the mountains on foot.

After leaving the police station, the group had stopped to buy clothes to replace what they'd lost. It was after nine when they finally made it back to Greville and the Ramblin' Ranch Hotel.

Not that things were much calmer there. One of the guests was in an uproar because he'd had his suitcase stolen. In all the confusion it had taken over an hour for the Hardys to check into their room.

But we made it, Joe thought happily. I'm finally getting my shower, and as soon as Frank comes back, we'll all go out for a big steak.

Joe was beginning to shrivel up from all the hot water, so he shut it off. As he wrapped himself in a large terry bath sheet, he heard the door click again.

"Frank? You back already?" he called, opening the bathroom door. Steam billowed out into the bedroom, but Joe could still make out the sneering face in front of him.

It was Bob Osmian, wearing a pair of ripped, filthy jeans, muddy hiking boots, and a clean shirt that was too small.

That wasn't the most noticeable thing about him, though. The most noticeable thing was the gleaming .38 revolver he held in his hand.

Chapter
Twenty-One

JOE DREW IN a deep breath. "Hey, watch where you're aiming that," he said lightly. "I'm glad to see you made it out okay. Say, nice shirt. Where'd you get it?"

"Borrowed it—and the gun—from an old gent down the hall," Osmian snapped. "Cut the chatter. I want my money, kid. Where is it?"

"Your money?" Joe knew Frank and Nancy had rehidden the suitcase up by the plane, but he wasn't about to tell Osmian that. Probably the FBI had recovered it already, anyway. "I don't know where it is."

The bookie's pale eyes narrowed to slits. "Look, don't play around with me. Either you tell me where the money is or I blow you away!"

Joe measured the distance between himself and Osmian. Could he jump him before the gun went off?

"Don't even think about making a move," Osmian said, his voice deadly. Joe decided he'd better heed the bookie's advice.

"This is nuts," Joe said. Maybe he could reason with the guy. "If you shoot me, everyone in this hotel will hear it."

"You think I care?" Osmian growled. "I got in here without anyone noticing, didn't I? This one-horse town is permanently asleep. I could be out through the window before anyone ever woke up enough to realize what happened."

He was probably right about that, Joe reflected uneasily.

Just then the door to the room rattled, as if someone was fumbling with a key in the lock. Frank! Joe thought. Talk about bad timing!

Moving like lightning, Osmian slipped behind the door. He cocked the revolver, then waved it at Joe. "Not a word," he whispered.

The door began to open. Joe tensed, ready to shout out a warning to Frank. He would just have to hope they could both duck out of Osmian's way in time.

"Coach!" Joe blurted out, doing a double-take as Pemberton stepped into the room.

The coach's rugged face was pale, and a long scrape marred one cheek. His damp, muddy clothing had rips all over it.

"What are you doing here?" Osmian demanded, stepping around the door to face the coach. "I told you to wait out of sight."

Coach shut the door wearily. "I can't go through with this," he said quietly. "It's wrong. I'm turning you in."

Joe stared from one man to the other. He couldn't quite believe what he was hearing. Was Coach Pemberton really giving up?

"What are you, crazy?" Osmian yelled. His face was purple with rage. "You're in this as deep as I am. Turn me in and you go down, too."

"That's right," the coach agreed with a sad smile. "I already called the cops. They're on their way."

"Why, you—" Osmian's lips twisted into a snarl, and he swung his gun around to aim it at Pemberton. He tightened his finger on the trigger.

"No!" Joe shouted. Moving faster than he'd known he could, he launched himself across the room and slammed into Osmian with a full body tackle. The gun went off as Osmian's hand flew up into the air, and the two of them crashed into the wall. Osmian's head cracked sharply against a wooden molding. He slid down the wall in an unconscious heap.

Breathing hard, Joe clambered to his feet and spun back around toward Coach Pemberton, who was leaning against the door, clutching his shoulder. A dark red spot was spreading on the sleeve of his blue work shirt, but he smiled at Joe.

"It's only a scratch. The bullet just grazed me," he explained. "Thanks to you."

"Wow, that was close," Joe said, letting out a long breath. Joe led the coach over to one of the twin beds and helped him to lie down. Then he went into the bathroom, wet a towel, and brought it out to press against the wound.

"I'd better call for an ambulance or something," he said. Joe dialed the emergency assistance number and alerted the reception desk, asking them to send up a first-aid kit. Then, seeing that Coach Pemberton's bleeding seemed to be under control, he pulled up a chair and sat down.

"So, tell me," he said after a moment. "How did you escape the rapids? Why did you decide to go straight?"

Coach Pemberton eased himself into a more comfortable position on the bed. "When the raft tipped, I kept my head and swam straight for the shore," he began. "Osmian must have had the same idea, because when I came up, he was right next to me—only he'd breathed in some water and was in bad shape. I pulled him out, and we hid in the woods until you kids got going again."

"But how'd you get through the fire?"

Coach stared vacantly into space above Joe's shoulder. Maybe he was replaying the escape in his mind. "I was pretty nervous," he admitted, "but I know those mountains pretty well. Actually, the fire wasn't spreading as fast as it looked, not after all the recent rains. I figured if we just kept close to the river, we'd have a good chance of getting through alive, and we wouldn't run into anyone, either. . . ." His voice trailed off.

"Go on," Joe prompted after a moment.

"Well, as soon as we got out, Osmian started talking about coming here to put the squeeze on you and your brother to get the money," Coach told him. "He made it pretty clear he intended to kill you to keep you quiet."

Joe sat up straight in the chair. "If no one ever found you or Osmian, it would go on record that you were both believed dead," he reasoned. "That way nothing could be traced to you. You could disappear and start somewhere else with a new identity." He shook his head in disgust, muttering, "Pretty sleazy, Coach."

Pemberton winced. "I won't blame you if you don't believe me when I say that I never expected things to go so far. But it's true. I never thought we'd resort to killing anyone."

He sighed, obviously ashamed. "Osmian was right about me, I didn't ask any questions. I just did what he told me and figured that if I didn't think about it, it wouldn't happen. But when he said he was going to kill you, I couldn't hide from the truth any longer. I've done a lot of awful things already—hurt the kids on my team and probably ruined my life." Coach made eye contact with Joe. "But this murder—I couldn't let it happen."

At that moment a loud knock sounded on the door. "State police," a voice called. "Open up."

Joe got up and went to the door. Just before opening it, he turned back to Coach Pemberton. "What you did was awful," he said. "But it took a lot of courage to give yourself up. I'm sure the court will take that into account."

"Well, I guess that's that," said George, sitting down on a padded bench in the hotel lobby the next morning.

"Yeah," Joe responded. He looked tired as he flopped down next to her. "Man, I got no sleep last night, what with that second trip to the police station to fill out a report on Coach Pemberton and Osmian. And I never did get a steak—much less a bacon cheeseburger!"

Nancy laughed and nudged Joe's sneaker with her foot. "But at least you caught the bad guys."

The three of them were waiting for Frank to finish checking out. In half an hour a van was due to arrive. It would shuttle all ten of the Wilderness Trek kids to the airport.

"It's odd," Nancy commented, twisting a strand of her reddish blond hair around her fingers. "We never did figure out who was behind some of the attacks on Johnny. I mean, we know that Coach Pemberton was behind the fire in George's and my room, and that he set up the fake obstacles for Johnny to clear—"

"But who sabotaged the carabiner?" George asked, picking up on Nancy's thought. "And who cut the rope when you guys fell into that crevasse?"

"We did put a major mob operation behind bars," Joe put in. "And that's something to be proud of." He smiled at Nancy and George, then said, "I never thought I'd say this, but since we all came out of this thing okay, I think you should just forget it."

Joe's blue eyes focused on something behind Nancy. Turning, she saw that Melissa and Stasia had entered the lobby, followed by Johnny. Johnny was carrying Melissa's backpack for her. "Put it down over there," she directed, pointing to a spot near Nancy, George, and Joe.

It figured that if only one backpack had been allowed on the helicopter, Melissa would make sure it was hers. Nancy glanced at George. George wasn't saying anything, but the pain in her eyes spoke loud and clear. Sighing, Nancy turned her attention back to Melissa.

The petite girl sat down and examined the fresh polish on her nails. "I can't wait to get back to civilization," she commented to Stasia in a loud voice. "This whole state is nowhere."

"I'll bet that girl wins prizes for charm and tact," Joe muttered.

Nancy hardly heard him, however. She was gazing at Melissa with narrowed eyes. Nail polish, she thought. Nail polish . . . What is it about nail polish that I should be remembering?

"That's it!" she murmured aloud.

George jumped, startled by Nancy's outburst. "That's what?"

Blinking, Nancy realized she probably wasn't making much sense to her friends. "Oh, nothing major," she said with a big grin. Then she held her hand up in front of her face and gazed critically at her fingernails. "Boy, this trip sure has mangled my manicure."

Now George was looking totally confused. "What manicure?" she asked. "Nancy, you haven't had a manicure in months!"

"Well, then, it's no wonder my nails look so lousy, is it?" Nancy replied lightly. "There's no time like the present to turn over a new leaf."

George turned to Joe and circled a finger around her temple. "I think this trip finally sent her over the edge," she said, rolling her eyes.

"Not at all," Nancy retorted. "In fact, I've

finally come to my senses about something I should have seen a long time ago."

Leaving George and Joe staring blankly after her, she walked over to where Johnny, Melissa, and Stasia were standing. Johnny smiled at her, but Melissa's eyes held nothing but hostility.

"Hi," Nancy said, greeting them. Turning to Melissa, she smiled politely and asked, "I noticed that clear nail polish you were using during our trek. Would you mind if I borrowed some?"

"What, you mean now?" Melissa asked dubiously.

Nancy gave a little laugh and said, "Well, my boyfriend's going to meet me at the plane, and I want to look my best when I see him."

Melissa raised an eyebrow. After a slight hesitation she unzipped her backpack, pulled out the bottle of clear polish, and gave it to Nancy.

"Thanks," Nancy told her, taking the little bottle. She unscrewed the top and lifted the brush to her nose.

A familiar, chemical scent filled her nostrils. Nodding with satisfaction, she resealed the bottle and handed it back to Melissa.

"Aren't you going to use it?" Stasia asked.

"I did use it," Nancy replied. "It already told me what I need to know."

Melissa made a face at Stasia. Her voice was

clearly annoyed as she asked, "What do you mean?"

"I think you know," Nancy told her. "It told me what I should have known from the beginning—that *you're* the one who's been putting the 'jinx' on Johnny!"

Chapter

Twenty-Two

THERE WAS a moment's shocked silence. Then Johnny slowly turned to face Melissa. "Melissa, is it true?"

Melissa's eyes burned with fury. "You nosy creep!" she shrieked, raising a hand to strike Nancy.

Nancy easily sidestepped Melissa's attack. As the girl flew past, Nancy grabbed her right arm and bent it up behind her back. Melissa gasped.

"Here, I'll hold her," Joe offered, stepping forward. He pinioned Melissa's arms to her sides, holding her easily in spite of her struggles.

The noise must have drawn the attention of others in the lobby, Nancy realized, because a second later Frank ran over, followed by Curt. "What's going on?" Frank demanded.

Nancy had been regarding Melissa steadily. Now, she explained, "Melissa's the one behind all those mysterious 'accidents' that kept happening to Johnny. I think she was trying to make him look like a jinx to the rest of us, though I'm not sure why. Maybe she can tell us," Nancy finished, fixing Melissa with another probing stare.

"Why should I tell you anything?" Melissa spat, her brown eyes flashing. "I'm not a dumb kid."

"That's true," Nancy said gravely. "In fact, the law may not view you as a dumb kid, either. You're seventeen, aren't you?"

Melissa nodded sullenly. "So?"

"So it's quite possible the courts will look on you as an adult and try you accordingly," Nancy replied. "You could be facing attempted murder charges. That's a lot of time in jail if you get convicted, you know."

"They wouldn't do that to me," Melissa said, but she didn't sound certain.

"They might," Joe told her.

Johnny still hadn't said a word—he seemed to be in shock.

Melissa's face crumpled. "I never really meant to hurt him," she said in a choked voice. "I just wanted to scare him a little."

A shocked murmur ran through the assembled teenagers. "Why?" Nancy asked quietly.

"He never—he never needed me," Melissa said brokenly. "Here he was, this big quarterback. I knew if I went out with him I'd be set. Everything would be perfect." She paused, her cheeks flushing. "I worked so hard to get him, but when I finally started going out with him— Oh, he always had other friends, other interests. I never felt like I came first with him. It made me mad."

"I don't believe this," Johnny muttered. "So you tried to kill me? You could have *talked* to me. Maybe we could have worked something out."

"I shouldn't have had to talk to you!" Melissa flashed. She jerked her head at Curt. "None of the other guys I ever went out with ignored me the way you did!"

"You were mad," Nancy interrupted gently. She wanted to get the conversation back on track. "So what did you do about it?"

Melissa swallowed before answering. "All these things had been happening to Johnny. I knew he already felt like bad luck was following him around. So I decided to help that along a little."

"You felt that the more insecure he felt, the more he'd come to depend on you," Nancy guessed.

"Uh-huh," Melissa replied, nodding. "I tried a couple of little pranks last year, like fixing the strap on his football helmet so it would come off while he was playing—"

"*You* did that?" Johnny gasped.

Ignoring him, Melissa went on. "It worked a little but not enough. So when I heard about this trip Coach was planning, I figured it would be the perfect opportunity to finish what I had started."

"You rigged Johnny's carabiner," Nancy said. "When he crossed that gorge, it snapped under his weight. He could have died in that fall!"

"I didn't know that would happen," Melissa protested, frightened. "I didn't even know what those little metal loops were for until Coach showed us how to use them that day at the gorge. By then it was too late. I just had to hope it wouldn't break and that he'd be okay."

She shivered. "I was terrified when he nearly fell. I never wanted to really hurt him!"

"If you never wanted to hurt him," George burst out, "then why did you pour kerosene all over his sleeping bag?"

"That's right," Nancy put in. "That was when I should have realized you were up to something. I saw you moving in your sleep, and then the fire shifted and Johnny's sleeping bag caught fire. But you weren't sleeping at all, were you? Because later you told Coach that you had seen George and me coming back from the woods."

"That fire wouldn't have hurt him," Melissa insisted. "I only put a few drops of kerosene on the bag—it was just for a little excitement. He got out without being harmed, didn't he?"

How could Melissa possibly think those kinds of pranks would make Johnny love her? Nancy caught Frank's eye, and he shook his head grimly. His expression said, This girl's got serious problems!

Johnny's voice brought Nancy's attention back to the group. "Even if I believe you about the fire and the carabiner," he challenged, "how do you explain the way my rope broke when we were crossing that ravine? If that wasn't an attempt to kill me, I don't know what is!" His face had lost its look of shock— now he was just plain angry.

"Don't say that! It wasn't meant for you, Johnny, it was meant for—" Melissa began. A strange expression suddenly flitted across her face, and she clamped her mouth shut.

Nancy leaned forward, instantly alert. "Go on, Melissa," she prompted. "Who *was* that cut rope meant for?"

Melissa's eyes wouldn't meet Nancy's. She kept silent.

Then the last piece clicked into place for Nancy. "Aha. That threw me off," she said thoughtfully. "I'd forgotten that all our ropes got mixed together that day after Coach Pemberton gave us that lesson in knots."

"Nan, what are you saying?" George asked, sounding horrified.

"It was *my* rope that you doctored, wasn't

it?" Nancy accused angrily. "*I* was the one who was supposed to suffer a fatal fall one day when we were rock-climbing. Johnny just happened to pick up my rope by accident. Is that it?"

Still Melissa said nothing. But Nancy saw that her whole body was trembling slightly.

"It makes more sense that way," Nancy went on. "You really didn't want to get rid of Johnny, but you didn't care about me. I'd been poking around, asking Curt questions about you, and you were getting nervous. So when you packed my backpack after breakfast that day, you took a minute or two to file away at my rope. You even had just the right tool along—your nail file. You bashed me on the head in the woods, too, hoping that would put me out of commission."

"Whoa!" Joe said softly. He tightened his grip on Melissa's arms.

"That was your big mistake," Nancy told Melissa. "Your nails were still wet with polish, Melissa, and some of it rubbed off on the rope. I smelled the nail polish on the rope, though I couldn't place it right away. It couldn't have been the pink polish, or I would have seen it, so it must have been the clear top coat that rubbed off." She jabbed a finger at Melissa as she added, "I'm sure a forensics lab will be able to identify it with no trouble."

Of course there was no way the rope *could* be examined, Nancy reflected. It had been abandoned with the rest of their stuff at the top of the mountain, but Nancy was hoping Melissa wouldn't remember that.

Suddenly tears brimmed in Melissa's eyes and poured down her cheeks. Pulling away from Joe she hunched forward and began to sob. "You're right! I didn't mean any harm," she choked out. "I just wanted Johnny to pay more attention to me."

Joe led her back to her seat and sat her gently down. "I guess this means another trip to the state police," he said in a resigned tone.

"Not necessarily," Nancy told him. "We only need to go to the police if someone presses charges against Melissa. And I don't plan to do that." She turned to Johnny. "Does anyone else want to press charges?" she asked as neutrally as she could.

Johnny looked startled. "What do you mean, you're not going to press charges?" he asked. "She tried to kill you! I'd think you, of all people, would want to see justice done."

"I do," Nancy told him. "But maybe there's a better way."

"Melissa needs help," Frank chimed in. Nancy was thankful that, as usual, he had understood what she meant. "She's not going to get it in prison, Johnny."

Johnny still looked undecided, though. Then Curt stepped forward and laid a hand on his arm. "Maybe all of us can help her, man," he said softly.

Curt and Johnny stared at each other for a long moment. Abruptly Johnny jerked his head in assent. "Okay," he said. "Let's try it your way."

"Well! Is it safe to say 'that's that' yet?" George asked, cautiously glancing around the tiny refreshment counter at the airport.

Nancy, Frank, and Joe all burst out laughing. "This time I think it is," Frank assured George, leaning against the counter.

They were the only ones of the group left at the airport. Dan and Pete had caught a plane to their home in Cincinnati, and the four Briarcliff students had all managed to squeeze onto a standby flight to Chicago. Frank and Joe weren't due to leave until later that afternoon, so Nancy and George had elected to wait with them.

"I still can't believe Melissa was the one doing all that stuff to Johnny," George marveled, taking a sip of her soda. "From the way she carried on every time something happened to him, I thought she really cared about him."

"I think she did, or does, in her own way," Nancy said thoughtfully. "I believe her when she says she didn't want to hurt him. She just didn't know where to draw the line."

Joe shook his head doubtfully. "I don't know about that," he said. "I hope you guys weren't too soft on her. Don't forget, Nancy, she did cold-bloodedly try to kill you."

"I'm not saying she isn't a seriously troubled person. It's just that I think there might be hope for her," Nancy told Joe earnestly.

"Speaking of hope . . ." Joe looked at George with a teasing glint in his blue eyes. "I saw you and Johnny talking very seriously just before he got on that plane. Is there any hope for the two of you?"

"Joe!" Frank protested. He punched his brother's arm lightly.

An embarrassed blush rose to George's cheeks, but she said, "No, it's okay. I don't mind answering that. I guess we'll just have to see," she said to Joe. "I told Johnny to look me up when he's gotten over this whole thing with Melissa."

Nancy put an arm around George's shoulders. "That was the best answer you could give."

After a moment of thoughtful silence Frank said, "You know, we really ought to come back here someday. I'd like to try this Wilderness Trek thing for real."

"Yeah, *without* all the extracurricular activities," Nancy agreed.

"Well, I'll only come on one condition," Joe warned the others. He looked solemnly from his brother to Nancy to George.

"What condition is that?" Nancy asked.

Suddenly Joe broke into a grin. "We eat nothing but bacon cheeseburgers!"